## Dedication

*This is for those who have always had a hard time choosing. Why pick one when you can have all three?*

*When everything goes to hell, the people who stand by you without flinching — they are your family.*

Jim Butcher

# Chapter

## ONE

T he familiar scent of stale beer and a hint of piss were the first things Adelynne Reid noticed as she walked up the street toward the bar she was supposed to meet her friend at. Well, maybe not her friend? They should have made it clear where they stood. She had met Dallas a few weeks before when she first moved into town.

⌁ℓℓ⌁

*Her old, unreliable car finally met its end on the interstate. The rusted, baby blue sedan had done what it could to bring Addie to a place of safety.*

*It was nearing midnight when the rumbling of a motorcycle stirred behind her. She furiously wiped away tears when she pulled her head off the steering wheel. A rapid knocking on her window drew her attention.*

*Adelynne had looked quite the mess as she eyed the biker. Their helmet was still on. Against her better judgment, she rolled down the window. Her beat-up ride had winding windows, and it took a moment or two before it was cracked halfway.*

"You okay, Honey Bee?" the sweet Southern accent breezed through her window. She was momentarily stunned, having assumed that the biker was a man. "I'm... I'm fine," Addie breathed out after a moment of silence, "I almost made it." Freedom. She was almost free.

The biker chick cocked her head in question. Her eyes were still hidden behind the visor on the helmet. If the girl in the car could see the worry clouding her eyes, she may have chosen better words. "Almost made it where Honey?" was all the biker girl asked.

The summer nights became more chilly as they inched closer to autumn. "I only had about 6 miles to go, and then I'd be at my motel," the hazel-eyed girl admitted.

Why was she still talking to this stranger? She didn't know. But something about the hidden girl made Addie never want to shut up.

"Are you staying at Ringer's? I can give you a lift and call someone to pick up your car for the night?" It was a nice offer. Tempting even.

"Yeah, that'd be nice, thank you..." Addie cut herself off, not knowing her name. "Dallas, the name's Dallas. And yours?". Addie smiled wide as the Southern accent made her feel all bubbly and safe, "my name's Addie."

"Addie, I like that. Addie." the other girl repeated as if to have the name become familiar on her tongue.

"Addie! Hello, Earth to Addie?" The smokey, Southern accent broke through her daze. The hazel-eyed stumbled to the side in her black-heeled boots. She had been unaware that her friend had been standing right before her for a few moments. "Dallas!" she screeched in excitement, pulling the petite girl into her arms.

Dallas' raven hair was down tonight. Her miraculous curls framed her lightly tanned face. Her light brown eyes were highlighted with the smokey eye makeup she wore.

Addie stepped back to take a good look over her friend. She wore an oversized band t-shirt for a rock band Addie hardly knew. The black shirt was cut down the middle far enough that Dallas' black lace bra was mostly on display.

She wore a pair of fishnets with black cowboy boots. She looked like a piece of Heaven in Addie's eyes. "You look amazing, Babe," Addie winked at her friend. No harm in light flirting between friends, right?

"Says you!" Dallas gushed as she took in Addie's outfit. The usually bright and cheery, maybe even innocent-looking outfits had been changed out for a more sexy look. The younger girl's closet didn't scream hot and sexy, but she was doing her best.

Addie grew shyer as Dallas' hungry eyes took in the girl before her. She pulled at the end of her too-short skirt. It was brown plaid, skin tight and hugging her curves in the best way. She was embarrassed by how tight it was on her stomach. Being a plus-sized girl came with a lot of shame. Most of it was instilled by those around her growing up.

She shook her head at those thoughts, not wanting them to ruin her night. She came out tonight for her first fun night here in Austin, Texas. Her long-sleeved black shirt perfectly accentuated her boobs, and her black-heeled boots clung to her thicker thighs. She looked like a slice of Heaven but was far from feeling like it.

Addie could already hear the old rock music blaring inside the bar. She squinted up at the neon sign. The red lights made up the words 'Tide Rising.' "Come on, let's get some drinks in us," Dallas chirped as she laced her fingers with Addie's, dragging the taller girl through the double doors. She momentarily stopped to kiss the one rough-looking guy's cheek before winking back at Addie.

She had never been to a biker bar before and didn't know what to expect. She had an idea but was still somehow caught off guard by the two dozen pairs of eyes that flicked to the two girls. She couldn't help but notice how the three men sitting at the end of the bar thoroughly checked her out. A blush rose to her cheeks before her face dropped. Why did she think they were even bothering to look at her while the smoke show of Dallas was right there next to her? That was definitely who they were checking out.

"Patriot, we'll take as many shots of tequila as you're allowed to pour us at once," Dallas giggled as another tough-looking guy stood at the bar. His large hands had been wiping down clean glasses with a microfiber towel. He was tall, and the deep amber hue of his skin was in stark contrast to his near-glowing grey eyes. He was a cool drink of water on a hot summer's day.

The man grunted, turning his eyes to the end of the bar before grabbing six shot glasses and placing them on the bar top. Without a word, the man turned around, holding the bottle of golden liquid. He pulled the lid off before pouring the shots for the two girls. Rock music continued to play in the background. It wasn't bad, but it wasn't precisely Addie's taste in music. It felt right in this place, like it belonged, unlike her.

Dallas grabbed two shots, nodding at Addie to do the same. "Cheers, bitch!" Addie couldn't help but shake her head at her friend. She grabbed two shots herself. The golden liquid burned as it went down her throat, but she didn't show that it even affected her. She heard Dallas cursing a bit beside her before taking her second shot.

Addie had no idea how it even happened. Still, somehow Dallas had convinced the bartender, Patriot, to let her pick the songs to play on the speakers. The two girls had cleared the floor by the left end of the bar. The two made it their dance floor.

Something was mumbled under his breath about the "damn MC Princess always getting her way," but Addie swore she could see a bit of a smile on the stone-cold man's face.

None of the men in the bar had dared to come close to the girls. Sitting back and watching in awe, the two girls ground on each other while singing their hearts out. There wasn't a man in the room who wasn't turned on by the sight.

The three men at the other end of the bar were watching on with darkened eyes. The biggest of the three's jaw clenched as he took in how many people were watching the girls. Instead of doing something about it, he just picked up his beer and took a swig as the man to his right tried to continue their hushed conversation.

Sweat was covering Addie and Dallas' exposed skin. The younger girl couldn't help but watch as Dallas' chest glistened under the bar lights. But no, she wasn't going to make a move on her first friend in this city, especially not after staring at the rock on her left hand. Not going to make that mistake.

Three shots turned into six for each girl, and Addie was beyond tipsy. She was a full-fledged drunk. She knew she'd wake up with a killer headache when the morning came, but she was having fun for the first time in a while.

This first taste of freedom made her heart clench. She was safe. She was happy. Addie had a fresh start at life and was going to make the most of it.

When the next song started playing, Addie lost it. One of her favourites. "I wanna have boobies!" Addie squealed as she danced, her hands running over her large breasts. She knew those weren't the lyrics, but they were all she ever heard when the song played. Dallas giggled as she copied Addie's dance for those lyrics, swinging her hips to the beat.

They truly were a sight to see. Dallas was known for turning the bar into her little party but never had anyone join her. Seeing her with a friend was a nice change. Tonight was something both of the girls had needed.

Alcohol flowed through them. Their coordination started to lessen as they stumbled a bit with their steps. A biker bar was a far step from being an actual club, with pool tables lining one side of the bar. Addie and Dallas were two of the handful of women in there tonight.

Addie had spotted a few girls older than her wearing jackets with 'Property of' patches that seemed to match what their men were wearing. She usually wasn't one to judge but felt it a bit odd to be referred to as property.

It was nearing two in the morning when a sexy song came on, and Dallas' eyes almost bugged out of her head. "Come on, Addie, let's give these boys a show!". The older girl climbed the barstool and gracefully hopped up on the bar top. Just like she's done a million times before. The men on that end of the bar moved their drinks closer to them as they looked up at the curly-haired girl.

A man with a patch that said "Prospect" on it held his hand out for Addie to help her up there too. Her friend was waiting, swinging her hips and dropping low before snapping back up. Addie hesitantly took the hand. A wobble in her step as her heels dug into the light cushion of the bar stool before stepping onto the bartop.

A quiet thank you, and a grateful smile were sent the man's way. He couldn't have been much older than her. Early 20s. He just smirked as he got a good look at her ass. On her way up, her skirt had ridden a little higher up her thighs, showing off her red lace panties.

As the song neared its end, Addie heard a "that's it" and a low growl behind her as a pair of strong arms wrapped around her waist, hoisting her down. Dallas wasn't too far behind her with a whine of "Cowboy!".

The fresh woodsy scent mixed with that of beer and whiskey invaded her senses as she felt her back land against a man's built chest. She let out a little scream as she felt herself near the ground, her eyes snapping shut, waiting to hit the hard, sticky floor.

But the harsh landing never came. "I'm not going to drop you," a dark voice muttered against her right ear. His scruff tickled her face. "Time for you and Dallas to go; too many eyes. I'm not about to tear them all out in one go," the unknown man said as he steadied Addie on the floor. One arm stayed around her waist, allowing the girl to stay up right. He needed to get her out of there.

"Allison Montgomery Caville, stop trying to fucking fight me," another deep, husky voice growled at her friend. Addie turned to look over at the tall man holding her friend hostage. His matching raven black hair and large beard were the only features she could make out besides his tattoos.

Addie fought against the man holding her as he dragged her away, trying to get to Dallas. "Let her go! Let me go!" Addie pleaded, her words slurring. She was really drunk.

The man holding Dallas chuckled as his bright blue eyes met Addie's hazel ones. "Cowboy, I can walk on my own," Dallas whined.

"I won't be surprised if Ghost turns your ass red for what you were just doing. As my sister, you get away with a lot of shit, but you had too many eyes on you," the man stated as he helped her to the door, "I'm sending Ghost home early."

Cowboy? Was this man her brother? "Oh God," she mumbled as she let the man, still holding her, bring her outside. She'd just made a fool of herself in front of Dallas' brother.

She was supposed to introduce Addie to Cowboy tomorrow. Dallas had invited her to a family dinner. And with how little money she had and no job yet, Addie wasn't passing up a free meal.

Bright red scattered across her cheeks as she was stopped right behind Cowboy. He seemed tense and heated as he spoke to the man Dallas had kissed on the cheek earlier. "Take her home, Ghost. No one touched her, but I'm sure some of the prospects had a good look at her panties," the man groaned.

Ghost, the bouncer, just looked at Dallas. A hint of amusement mixed with something darker filled his eyes. Addie couldn't make out what it was.

"What about Addie?" Dallas asked, looking over Cowboy's shoulder at her friend.

"We've got her. We'll take her home. You just focus on not falling off the back of Ghost's bike". And that was the end of the conversation as Ghost took his drunk fiancee away and over to the row of bikes, climbing on one as Dallas followed suit.

Addie was now left alone with Cowboy and two other men; the man behind her finally drew his arm away from her. She wrapped her own arms around her stomach as she looked up at the tall men around her. The only person she knew had just bailed on her, and she was left here to face the wolves.

"Let's get you home, Addie. It's cold out," Cowboy said quietly as he looked at the other two men. "I can call a cab like I did to get here," she didn't know why, but she wasn't scared of these men even though it looked like she should be. They were all taller than her and looked incredibly strong. They were covered in tattoos except for their faces.

"Prez, I can wait with her, and you can go back in," the remaining bouncer said genuinely as he looked at the man to Addie's right. "She's Dallas' friend, and she'll have our heads if we let her take a cab right now. Who knows what could happen to her," he replied coolly before walking towards a black truck. He was cocky enough to know she'd follow behind like a lost puppy. It managed to feed the growing smirk on his face.

Maybe she lacked common sense or self-preservation, but she followed the three men to the black truck parked on the street. With each step forward, Addie's eyes grew heavier.

The remaining man hadn't said a word to her. Opening the back door for Addie, he helped her into it. She quietly thanked him, her eyes meeting his chocolate brown ones.

"Tsk tsk tsk," he started, "such a pretty thing like you ending up in our truck, not even a little bit scared. Maybe you should be," he said before shutting her door. His and Ginger's accents didn't fit in around here, confusing Addie. But she guessed her accent wasn't from around here, so she couldn't judge.

Addie watched as Cowboy climbed into the seat beside her, closing his door behind himself. The red-haired one climbed in the front seat while the scary one climbed in the passenger seat. Cowboy had distracted Addie, sliding her seatbelt into place. The click of the child lock going on was covered by the seat belt clicking into place.

"Where to, Adelynne?" the driver asked. How'd he know her first name? She couldn't be bothered to ask. "Ringer's Motel," she stated politely before looking out the window. She couldn't keep up with his hardening stare through the rearview mirror. He grunted in response before turning onto the road.

It felt like a much longer drive to the motel, but she managed to doze off. She didn't even notice Cowboy covering her with his leather jacket.

Something about the curvy girl was intriguing to the three men. She wasn't scared of them even after what Ruger had said to her. "She has no self-preservation, does she?" Boston grumbled when he noticed she was out cold. He turned the opposite way onto the highway, heading towards their home.

What was he doing? This was just some friend of Dallas'. He should be dropping her off at the motel. He couldn't allow himself to get attached. Bad things happened when Boston got attached to a woman. He vowed never to let it happen again.

"Bos, are you sure about this?" Addie heard Cowboy ask as she was lulled to sleep by the truck's movement. "No," was all that was said in response.

# Chapter
## TWO

**S**weat beads rolled down Addie's face. She knew she was going to be sick. She pulled herself from the tangled sheets, slipping her bare feet onto the floor. The coolness from the hardwood floor sent shivers through her body.

Taking in the dark room, Addie saw that there was an en suite bathroom to her left.

In a hurry, she rushed to the bathroom. She barely reached her knees before hurling up last night's drinks and her dinner. Throwing up was one of Addie's worst fears. Hearing the sounds bounce off the walls made it worse to the point she was now dry-heaving. Everything in her stomach had already come up.

Tears ran down her face as she did her slow breathing. It was a few moments before she shakily stood up. Without another look in the bowl, she flushed the toilet. She rummaged in the drawers under the sink and luckily found an unopened toothbrush.

She didn't know where she was, not even remembering how she got here. Maybe she went to Dallas' house after the bar? Her memory of last night's activities were mostly hazy.

Looking in the mirror after brushing her teeth, Addie realized that her makeup had smudged around her eyes. There was only so much she could do to not look like a raccoon. Where was she?

As she returned to the bedroom, she could hear men yelling from the hallway. Their feet moved faster, stomping their way down the hall. Their heavy boots hitting wood drove anxiety straight into Addie's chest. She looked around wide-eyed.

Her first instinct was to hide. But where? Closet? Classic, she'd be killed instantly. Horror movie-type death. Bathroom? They'd find her too quick. There was also no way she was fitting under the bed.

All she had left was to fight. When her eyes landed on a gun on top of the dresser next to a wallet, she praised whatever Gods were above for taking pity on her.

Panic filled her facial features as she grabbed the black weapon. With shaking hands, she held it facing the ground to her right. She could do this. At least, that's what she told herself.

The room no longer smelled like mint and sandalwood; instead, in its place was the smell of stale cigarettes and the pungent smell of body odour. The scent rolled through Addie's stomach. Her hangover was not helping the situation.

The footsteps halted in front of the bedroom door. The handle jiggled as it was turned. "Goodmor-" Dallas' voice cut off as she peeked around the man before her. His tan skin and tattoos were on display in his tight t-shirt. His chocolate brown hair was slicked back. It was obvious he had just gotten out of the shower as a few drops of water rolled down his neck from his wet hair.

He wore a cocky smile on his face. His dimples became deeper as he took in the sight before him. Addie was shakily holding the gun pointed right at him. He cocked his head to the side before he chuckled darkly.

"Baby, if you're going to point a man's own gun at him, make sure it's loaded first," he growled before taking three steps forward. His left hand wrapped around the end of the gun, pulling it towards himself while peeling Addie's hands away with his right hand.

Tears grew in her eyes, and a gasp came from her throat like she had finally gotten her head above water again. "I'm so sorry!" she sputtered. The rancid smell of body odour and cigarettes were long gone, gone like a distant memory. She wasn't trapped in that Hell anymore. She was safe.

"That was kind of badass," Dallas said after a moment of silence, "didn't take you for pulling a gun on someone," she admitted.

Addie could now see the two other men who had followed in behind the others. "I heard yelling and boots hitting the ground,"

Addie rubbed at her face, her hands still shaking, "I didn't know where I was."

"You were pretty drunk last night," the Southern, dark-haired man chuckled. Cowboy. Addie vaguely remembered that he was Dallas' brother. "This asshole promised he'd get you to your motel, but of course, he lied and brought you here," Dallas gave her brother a dirty look. The man raised his hands in defence. "You take that up with Boston; he's in charge here."

Cowboy had nodded back at the long-haired, ginger, Greek God of a man with a smug look. His eyes, a dark emerald colour, stared back at Addie's hazel ones.

Dallas hadn't said another word knowing better than to start a fight with Boston. He was the Rising Tide's president. No one was stupid enough to fight him. They knew he meant business.

"I'm sure you're hungry," Cowboy started, a soft look on his face, "we need to get some water and pain meds into you. I'm sure you're beyond hung over". Dallas' eyes flicked between her friend and her brother. A small frown appeared on her face before she masked it.

"Yeah, come on, Addie, I'll show you to the kitchen!" Dallas put on her charming smile before striding over and grabbing her friend's hand. Addie willingly let the smaller girl drag her out of the room.

They were at the end of a long hallway, a door on each side and the end. There were a handful of other bedrooms as they continued down the hall. It felt like they were in a frat house to her. How many bedrooms did someone need? They neared the staircase, and Addie mentally prepared herself not to trip down the stairs as Dallas dragged her.

Something was odd about this place, but she couldn't quite put her finger on it. She didn't have much time to dwell on it before she found herself parked on a stool in the kitchen. The stool was very similar to the ones at the bar, she noted to herself.

Addie noticed that the guys hadn't followed them into the kitchen, and she was able to take a deep, calming breath. "Is this your house?" she asked Dallas curiously.

"No, silly, this is the clubhouse. My brother and his friends live here with a few other members," she informed. That caused many more questions to form. From the quizzical look on Addie's face, Dallas took pity and slumped forward on the kitchen island. Her elbows were placed on the cool stone, her hands holding her head up. "Didn't I explain that my brother, his friends and my fiance are bikers?"

"Like, dirt biking as a sport or hobby?" she was confused. She became even more confused when Dallas burst out laughing at her response. "No, Honey Bee, like MCs."

"You're going to have to explain better than that…" Addie mumbled. "They're part of a motorcycle club. Boston is the president or leader, and Cowboy, my brother, is the vice president. Ruger, the one you had a gun pointed to, he's the sergeant at arms. And my fiance, Ghost, he's an enforcer," Dallas said cheerfully.

"Why were you all yelling before you broke into the room I was in? Whose room was it anyway?"

"I was annoyed that the boys ruined our fun last night and then didn't even take you back to your motel as they had promised. I went to your room this morning and panicked when you wouldn't pick up the phone or answer the door," Dallas admitted, "I called Cowboy in tears, and he said you were fine and asleep in Ruger's room."

Addie's cheeks blushed a bit, remembering the night before. "We were a mess last night, Dal." "At least we looked hot," she winked, "Ghost couldn't get enough of me last night. My ass is probably still red and hot".

That confused Addie; it was evident on her face. "He spanked me," Dallas explained as she licked her lips, "his hands are delicious."

"But you're not a child? Is he hurting you? I can help you get out; just say the word".

Dallas howled with laughter, "he's not hurting me, Honey Bee. I love it. I'm sure if you found someone with a nice pair of hands and a dominant personality, you'd enjoy a spanking or two yourself".

Addie scoffed at that, but the happiness radiating from her friend made her stop from continuing this conversation. She already did what she could. She offered the girl a way out, and if she wasn't going to take it, it was not Addie's problem.

She quickly took the pain meds and water Dallas had offered but mostly stayed quiet. She noticed she was still dressed in her outfit from the day before. A feeling of shame came with that recognition, but she pushed it down.

"So, what do you say?" Apparently, Dallas had been talking to her. She hadn't even heard her friend. "I'm sorry. What did you ask?".

"We're having a family dinner tonight. Would you like to come and meet everyone?". Dallas looked hopeful but bit her lip in anxiety. She didn't want Addie to turn her down. "It's just the guys, some of their old ladies will be here. You'll love them! Boston said something about making burgers on the grill tonight for it".

"Old ladies?". "Yeah, that's what we call the girls who are with one of the MC guys. For example, I'm Ghost's old lady," she replied proudly. "But you're not old," Addie pointed out. "It's just a saying, Honey Bee."

"Okay, I'll come. I should be heading out now. I'm itching to get out of this outfit," she admitted.

After Dallas and Addie's goodbyes, Addie found her heeled boots and purse. She gathered her things before stepping outside.

Her rideshare made sure to get her back to her motel in one piece. Her morning was chaotic, to say the least. She couldn't believe she pulled a gun on a man. She also couldn't get the looks on the men's faces or how hard they had gotten from that scene.

A shiver ran down her spine. What was going on? She didn't know if she wanted to find out what that meant.

Addie didn't have much to her name, leaving most of it behind when she left. All she had was a backpack filled with her important items. She'd bought a cheap phone on her second day in Austin, but besides that, she only had a few outfits, her stuffed teddy bear, a pair of heeled boots, and a pair of black canvas shoes.

Addie got dressed in her light green dress with a soft blue floral print. The dress had spaghetti straps and strings tied together, lying in the middle. On top of the dress, she wore a light cream cardigan. She sat on the edge of the crappy bed she's been sleeping on lately, pulling her black canvas shoes on her feet one at a time.

Her makeup from last night had been washed off, replaced by a light, neutral look with a cherry pink lip stain. Her hair was pulled back in a half ponytail, soft curls falling down her back. She was nervous about making a better second impression knowing she had blown her first.

As her rideshare approached the building she had spent the previous night in, her insides started to bubble with nerves. She said goodbye to the driver before her feet touched the gravel driveway. The building was out of town, surrounded by trees. Private. Very private.

Motorcycles were lined up neatly beside each other. This must be some big family.

She could hear laughter and people talking from the side of the building. She followed the noises and was surprised to see how many people were at this "family event."

She spotted Dallas curled up on the lap of the bouncer from the other night. Ghost was his name, Dallas' fiance. An enforcer. Whatever that meant. They were sitting around a bonfire. The crackling of wood sounded in the air.

Her eyes drifted around as she took everything in. She spotted the three men she went home with the night before standing around a grill with bottles of beer in their hands. It looked like they were having an intense conversation.

Addie saw a few kids running around with a frisbee. They laughed loudly as they played. They were completely carefree, and it warmed the girl's heart. It also made her frown.

She took a deep breath before tearing her eyes away from the little boy that looked about four years old.

Guilt ate at her. A war raging inside Addie. She looked torn when Cowboy's eyes snapped to hers. Something about his cold blue eyes felt inviting. It was odd. She offered the man a small wave. She was awkward and about to cave inward when Cowboy motioned for her to come over.

Her feet moved across the grass of their own free will. Moving her towards the three men.

When Addie reached the three men, their conversation came to an end. "I don't think we introduced ourselves last night or this morning," Cowboy admitted. Addie's hands clasped in front of her, a sign of anxiety. "I'm sorry about this morning. I'm so embarrassed".

"Nonsense. You didn't know where you were," the long-haired ginger said casually, "you also wouldn't be the first to pull a gun on Ruger here. Well, maybe the first woman to..." he trailed off, a growing smirk appearing on his face.

Ruger, the man Addie had a gun pointed at this morning, only grunted in response. He was a man of few words at the moment. His eyes were dark, and he barely acknowledged Addie's existence. The beer bottle in his hand was raised to his mouth.

"As warm and snuggly as Ruger's being, we should properly introduce ourselves," Cowboy said as he patted Ruger's shoulder. "I'm Cowboy, Dallas' older brother. The tall, sexy ginger is Boston, and Mr. Grumpy-pants is Ruger. What's your name, sweets?".

"Adelynne, but you can call me Addie." Why was she blushing? She's going to make a fool of herself.

"Addie, what a sweet name," Cowboy nearly cooed. His sweet, Southern tang made her heart skip a beat or two.

Cowboy asked Addie many questions, from simple ones like how long she's known Dallas to whether she was still feeling the effects of last night's drinking. He managed not to bring up the gun incident.

That's what she was calling it—the incident.

Boston and Ruger seemed to be talking amongst themselves as Boston continued grilling. Yet she could still feel their eyes flicking back to her like they were watching what was going down with Cowboy.

When Addie first arrived, Cowboy handed her a beer. She would take a sip here and there, mostly out of nervousness. She knew Dallas knew she was here. The shorter girl was still curled up with her man by the fire.

Addie wouldn't say she's shy. She was just quiet in new situations. She liked to watch and see what would happen rather than approach others she didn't know. That's probably why she had minimal friends.

"Brown Eyes!" a man called out as he approached the four by the grill. Addie recognized him as the man that helped her onto the bar last night. He was wearing the same leather jacket as the previous night, the one that said 'Prospect' on it.

Was that his name? Addie couldn't help but wonder. All the men seemed to have weird names around here. Maybe it was a Texan thing. She didn't quite understand.

"Nice to see you again, Brown Eyes," the man smiled cheerfully, "I didn't get a chance to talk to you before you got kicked out. I went out after you, but you were gone".

"I'm sorry, are you talking to me?" She was confused, "my eyes are hazel..." she added.

She felt an arm wrap around her waist. She was being tugged into somebody's side. Addie watched as the man before her eyes widened. He stuck his hands up in surrender. "Didn't know she was yours, Prez," and before he could say another word, the man turned on his heel and walked away, shaking his head.

Why had Boston done that? Maybe the guy was a sleazeball. Maybe Boston was just trying to be helpful. With the way everyone was looking at them with Boston's arm still wrapped around her waist, he may as well have pissed on her. He was acting like he was claiming his territory.

Later on in the evening, Addie found herself around the fire with Dallas across from her. The two girls were giggling and talking about their night before. Ghost didn't seem mad about their antics the previous night. He chuckled along to their stories. His large hand was splayed out on Dallas' thigh. She was still perched on his lap.

Addie couldn't help but feel butterflies as she recalled this morning. Ghost had spanked Dallas. Dallas liked it.

Addie had never thought she'd be into someone spanking her before now, but maybe something about Ghost's protective hand on his woman was changing her thoughts.

"Thank you for coming and meeting the family," Dallas said as their conversation started to die out. Addie's bright smile shone through. "Thank you for inviting me. I had a great time".

"I'm sure we'll see you around here more often," Ghost had added. His eyes seemed to linger behind Addie's head. She turned to look over her shoulder, seeing the three men she had spent most of the day with looking at them. "I'm sure Cowboy already has plans to keep you here forever," Dallas rolled her eyes. She didn't seem too pleased with her brother at the moment.

Addie flinched at her tone. Was her friend mad at her? "I'm sorry." What else could Addie even say? Ghost's hand squeezed Dallas' thigh. Dallas knew she was being silly. "No, I'm sorry," Dallas sighed, "you're just my first friend in a while, and I'm not good with sharing."

Ghost turned his head back to face Addie. "Cowboy does like you."

*"Cowboy does like you."* It replayed in her mind over and over again. Part of her wondered if Boston liked her too. She shrugged it off. She was being silly. People who looked like that could never want someone who looked like her.

Her chest constricted under the grip of those thoughts. Worthless. That's how she always felt. She would always be on her own. She felt at home with her loneliness.

# THREE

S ummer was supposed to be the best time of the year—the perfect weather for pool parties and beach visits. Instead of having fun like others her age, Addie's feet were pounding the pavement as she tried to secure a job.

The small amount of money she had started her new life with would only last so long. She tried to prepare for this. No one seemed to want to give her a try. With no previous jobs or experience, Addie was doing what she could to get ahead in life.

She was dressed in a pair of light blue, ripped skinny jeans. A basic red tank top covered by a cream chunky cardigan with red strawberries on it. Her black canvas shoes were tucked on her feet.

The summer sun beat down on her as she roamed the streets of Austin. It was draining. So mentally draining for her to be told no everywhere she went. She had no money to get to a busier part of the city. She could only get somewhere by foot, and being on the outskirts of Austin meant there were fewer opportunities for employment.

She needed a car but couldn't get one until she had money. It was a vicious cycle. No job meant no money, which meant no car, which meant she couldn't find a job.

The silver bell above the door rang as she walked into the pharmacy. She was ecstatic to see a 'help wanted' sign plastered on the dirty window.

The pharmacy was family-owned. It didn't look like a big company. It was small, and the aisles were crowded. Only one person could fit through the row at a time.

The linoleum floors hadn't been maintained, with cracks and chips in almost every tile. Dust littered every surface as far as her eyes could see. The musty scent permeated the air.

These were all good signs to Addie; maybe these people were desperate enough to give her a shot.

Addie walked up to the front counter and saw a teenage boy leaning against the cabinet. His phone was in his hands, not even looking up momentarily as she approached.

"Good morning," she started kindly. The boy barely acknowledged her. He was more interested in the messages he was typing out. "I saw that you were hiring. Is there someone I can speak with about a job?"

The brown-haired boy looked up at Addie. He shook his curls before moving the hair from his face. "Sorry, my mom isn't here, but if you leave your resume, I'll give it to her."

"I don't have a resume," Addie braced herself. After being turned down by a handful of businesses, she knew what was coming next. "Oh," the boy replied. Addie watched as he scratched his head awkwardly, "My mom kinda needs those to go over your experience before an interview."

*Don't cry. Do not cry.* She repeated to herself in her head. Addie took a deep breath in, centering herself. "Thank you, I hope you have a good day." She turned on her heel and walked back out the door without another word.

This was starting to become embarrassing. She willed the tears away as she continued down the street.

Addie noticed a pop can lying on the ground. Her canvas shoe kicked at it as she walked. The metallic noise of the can bouncing and scraping against the ground was welcomed. She needed a distraction.

She didn't know what she could do. Why was she such a failure? He had been right. She'd never make it alone; she would always need someone to care for her.

Bile rose up her throat at that thought. She pushed it away. She wouldn't think of him. She was supposed to be free but knew she'd never be free from the memories.

Sleep didn't come easy nowadays. She had done her best to cover her dark circles. Her daily reminder was that she was running out of time and not doing enough. Addie felt like her luck was running out.

She had managed to escape while he was asleep; he didn't even know she had left. His beer bottle had fallen from his hand, smashing against the hardwood floors.

She remembers the panic in her chest as she carefully walked by the couch. She had been terrified to wake him up.

He had always slept deeply, but she needed to ensure her escape plan would work. She was lucky it did, but it seemed her luck was about to run out. She had no one to turn to, nowhere else to run. She was without a car or money. She had nothing but what she could carry on her back.

The late summer heat was starting to get to her. She was hot, tired and stressed out. Addie knew she had a number of days before she was out on the streets. Her fresh start was supposed to be filled with rainbows and butterflies; instead, it was filled with pain and misery.

She was tired. Every day she was becoming more and more tired of everything. The only person she trusted in this city was Dallas. She missed her friend.

It's not like Dallas didn't try to stay in contact with her, but Addie had refused to reply. She didn't want to make this any harder than it was. Her happiness would always be short-lived.

Addie didn't want to become more attached to Dallas than she was. Life was a disaster. She wasn't sleeping because she was too busy searching the Internet for work. When she did sleep, it was minimal due to the nightmares that plagued her.

Maybe she shouldn't call them nightmares; they were more like not-so-distant memories. Memories of the life she was trying to run away from.

The local grocery store was her next stop. The bright lights flickered like they were barely holding on. Much like she was.

The produce section was small and barren, with only some apples and oranges. A few oranges had fallen from where they were set up, stopping a few feet away. Besides the few oranges on the floor, the store was pristine.

After speaking with one of the employees in the cereal aisle, Addie was led into a back office. A heavy-set man sat behind a cluttered desk. Papers were strewn about. She could smell the scent of stale cigarettes on his breath and did her best to breathe through her mouth.

"So I hear you're looking for a job?" the man started. His South-ern accent wasn't nearly as sweet as Dallas' or as attractive as

Cowboy's. "Yes, and I can start immediately." She hoped to come off as excited to work but knew it was coming across as desperate.

The man looked at her with a frown. "I'm not looking for some sort of charity case. I have enough problems to deal with here already." Could he hear her heart shattering within her chest?

"I'm willing to do grunt work, really; whatever you need to be done around here, I'll do!" Begging. She's resorted to begging and bartering. Four days. She only had enough money to make it four more days. She was running out of time quickly.

His resounding "no" echoed through the room.

Addie thanked the man for his time before making her way back through the store and to the outside world. She needed a breath. She needed someone to give her a break.

Tears rolled down her cheeks as she walked silently down the road. She was sure it would have come up by now if she had anything in her stomach this morning. Her anxiety had a death hold on her. The nausea overwhelmed her.

The sound of children's laughter carried its way from the park she walked by. Addie wiped at her tired eyes as she looked over to see the children playing.

The world was cruel. People were cruel.

She carried so much anger within her. Her skin itched as these feelings continued to grow.

Why couldn't she be like them? Carefree and happy.

The remainder of her first summer living in the outskirts of Austin, Texas, flew by. She had spent every waking moment of the last two weeks making her final push for employment.

Addie had applied at the local library, the middle school down the road, and even the post office. She either didn't have the right education or just lacked experience.

How could someone without a work history gain experience if no one was willing to give her a chance? She wasn't even lucky enough to get an interview. When she couldn't produce a resume, she was turned down immediately.

Addie could barely keep her motel room in her name. It was becoming too expensive. The owner had taken pity and only charged her half the normal rate, but it wasn't enough. She'd be without somewhere to live in four days if she couldn't find a job.

She had no car, no home of her own. Why did she think she could do this? That she could escape her bad luck?

She did the only thing she could do. The only place she hadn't applied to. Her last chance.

She walked the hour-long trek toward Tide Rising. She was nervous. What if Dallas was there? She'd blown off her friend's plans for weeks now. Avoiding her. She knew her happiness here wouldn't last. It never did.

She looked so out of place as she neared the bar. She needed to do this. She needed a job.

There wasn't a bouncer in sight when she arrived. It wasn't surprising as it was only nearing 2:00 pm on a Thursday. She had checked the hours online before making her trek over, so she knew they were open.

Reaching out, she pulled open the front door, stepping inside. She knew she stuck out like a sore thumb. She knew immediately when the customer's eyes had wandered over to her. She wasn't going to let anything stop her. She needed this.

Relief flooded over her when she recognized the bartender. Patriot. He was the one serving drinks on her first night here.

Addie walked up to the bar. She wore a warm smile as she approached. "Good afternoon, Patriot." Be polite, be kind.

The bartender narrowed his eyes at her before looking behind her like he was looking for someone. There was no one behind her. "What can I help you with?".

"Is there a manager or someone I can speak with? I'm looking for a job".

For a moment, Patriot was stunned. He shook himself out of it before grabbing a glass, filling it with ice and water, and placing it in front of Addie. "Sit. I'll be back. Don't talk to anyone, don't look at anyone".

It was a warning.

So she sat on the leather stool, sipping on the cool water. How'd he know she was thirsty? Was she sweating badly from her walk? She must be. Now she was even more embarrassed. She hugged her arm around her stomach, trying to make herself appear smaller.

"And you just left her out here?" she heard a man grumble from her right. "I gave her water, told her to stay, and immediately got you. You don't need to cut my balls off for this," Patriot replied as he threw his hands in the air in exasperation.

The sound of boots coming closer was what made Addie turn. She noticed Boston a moment before he placed his left hand on her lower back. "Let's go somewhere more private," Boston told her, "you can bring your drink too."

"Oh, sorry, Boston, but I can't. I'm waiting to speak with someone about a job".

"I know, Adelynne. That's why I invited you to my office". Oh.

She was really making a fool of herself. Boston's hand lay possessively on her lower back as he led them to an office by the bathrooms. Once they were closed in the room, she felt heat coming off her in waves.

Boston strolled around the side of the desk before settling in his chair. He pointed to one of the two leather chairs in front of his desk, requesting she sit down. The room was small. It held a desk, two chairs in front of it and a small couch to the side.

"I'll start by telling you we weren't looking to hire anyone," he started as he took a good look over the girl. She had dark circles under her eyes, and he could tell she had lost some weight since they last saw each other at the bbq. He didn't like this. Didn't like that this girl was suffering.

"I'll do anything you need. I'll clean and peel gum from under the bar and tables. I can be a bouncer if needed," she nearly pleaded. She needed a chance.

"Even if I had a security position available, I wouldn't hire you for it," Boston stated matter-of-factly.

That stung. "I know I don't have experience, but I can do it. I've handled a lot of drunks in my lifetime. I can do it". She'd do whatever he needed her to do. This was her only hope.

"It's not the experience that concerns me. It's the fact you would be put in harm's way," the man sighed. He ran his hand through his long hair. He looked stressed. Conflicted even.

"A job's a job," Addie muttered, feeling defeated.

"Where have you been, Adelynne? Dallas is worried sick about you". Boston pulled his hand from his hair before placing his elbows on his desk. Addie looked cute in her little outfit. She looked soft. Innocent. Yet, it was still an odd outfit for the late summer heat.

"I've been spending every day trying to find a job. You'd think there'd be more opportunities with a city this big. But no, everyone wants experience," she was getting increasingly frustrated as her time was ticking. "How am I supposed to get experience, Boston? If no one will give me a chance?" Oh, here came the tears.

Addie turned her face to the ceiling, trying to reign them in. She felt like she was drowning. She'd be homeless in four days with nothing to her name besides the backpack her belongings were in. She had nothing of value to sell. She was stuck.

A knock sounded at the door, but Addie paid it no mind. Her lip wobbled as she tried not to cry. She needed to be strong. That's all she had left, her strength.

A quiet "come in" from Boston came. She heard the door open, and two pairs of footsteps followed into the small office. Addie didn't look.

A fool. She was a fool. Boston hadn't even cared to reply to her comment.

One of the people that came in walked over to the small couch against the left wall, taking a seat. The other took a seat in the second leather chair.

"Sweets, come here," the sweet, Southern drawl sounded from beside her. Cowboy. She didn't know why she did it. Maybe she just needed some form of comfort. But she got up, walking over to where Cowboy was seated.

"Up," he commanded lightly. He wanted her on his lap. She shook her head no as more tears formed, a cry bubbling in her throat. "Too big," she cried out. He wasn't taking that. He grabbed her by the back of her thighs, pulling her to where he wanted her.

As soon as she was situated on his lap, her knees on either side of his thighs, she lost it crying. Cowboy held her close. He nuzzled her neck with his nose as he held her close. His large hands rubbed against her back as he shushed her.

Ruger and Boston watched as the younger girl cried into Cowboy's shoulder. Boston's hands itched to hold her the same way, but he knew he couldn't. He needed to keep some distance from her. He was already too protective of her.

As soon as Patriot told him that his Adelynne was sitting in the bar asking for a job, he called Ruger and Cowboy. She didn't know it yet, but she was theirs and needed their protection. He knew something was going on.

"She's not working here," Ruger muttered, a tinge of anger hidden within his words. "Unless you can take her at the shop or Cowboy takes her. It seems she's run out of options," Boston replied as he watched Addie's shaking shoulders.

"I don't think a tattoo shop or a mechanic will be any better than here at the bar," Ruger was shaking his head. He knew the clientele for the three businesses. He knew they could be ruthless, and Addie was soft; she couldn't handle it. Dallas had to learn how to take it, but she was untouchable. She was Cowboy's sister and Ghost's fiance.

Besides Boston's claim at the get-together, nothing stopped someone from trying something with Addie. Ruger didn't like that. Neither did Boston or Cowboy.

"She's lost weight, dark circles under her eyes..." Boston pointed out, "Cowboy said her lights are on most of the night. She should be sleeping, but she's not".

Addie drew her head back from Cowboy's shoulder. She'd heard a bike come late at night and leave early in the morning. It couldn't be. Why was Cowboy there?

Cowboy's eyes were soft when Addie's reached them. "You've been checking up on me?".

"Of course," he nodded, "you've been ours from the moment we met."

Ours.

*Ours.* That word hung in the air. "You're ours, Addie," Cowboy continued, "the moment we saw you walk into the bar with Dallas, we knew."

"Dallas had already talked our ears off about you before that night," Ruger said with a roll of his eyes. "The moment you walked in, you became part of the family. You'll be protected as such. If you're in trouble, the club will back you up," Boston explained, "you're our responsibility now. The club's responsibility".

Oh. That's what he meant. Not theirs. But the club's. She inwardly sunk before untangling herself from Cowboy's hold. Addie situated herself back in her chair. She used the sleeves of her cardigan to clean up any remaining tears.

"Sorry, Cowboy, for the tears and stuff," her cheeks bright red. "Not the first time a pretty girl cried on my shoulder, and probably not the last," he mused.

"So about this job..." she trailed off, changing the subject.

"There are some odd jobs that the three of us could use you for if you're willing to do them," the oldest man explained, "they're simple jobs. You'll be paid cash at the end of each shift".

"You can help me by answering the phone and doing some office duties at the body shop I own," Cowboy explained, "my normal assistant is in college and can't do Monday through Wednesday anymore due to school."

"I could use some help Thursday and Friday nights at my tattoo shop," Ruger admitted, "those nights are too busy for me to keep up with everything, and then I hate cleaning up the mess on Saturdays."

"If you want to pack your schedule, I can use your help here on Saturdays and Sundays," Boston said.

"I'll do anything. I won't let any of you down. I don't even care how much you want to pay me. I just need to pay $350 weekly to keep my room." Addie was so giddy. She not only got one but three jobs. These three men were giving her a shot.

A pained look crossed Boston's face. "I know you don't have a car, Adelynne, and I don't feel comfortable with you staying in that motel much longer. Cowboy found some shady characters around there the last few weeks."

"Oh, it's fine. It's only until I can save up enough money for three months' rent." Addie knew that it'd take her a while in this city, but she would do it. She was going to make a home here.

"How about an alternative?" Addie's ears perked up at that. "How about you stay in one of our spare rooms?" The blonde asked. Before Addie could refuse, knowing she had too much pride. "$200 for a week's rent. Food, internet and travel to and from work included. You'll save at least $150 a week by doing this. Then you can get your own place quicker".

Ruger and Cowboy's eyes nearly bugged out of their heads at that. Addie nodded as she considered it. "Okay, but I have to help pay for gas. That's the only way I'll say yes." What could it hurt?

"Fine, you can help pay for gas," he nodded as his hands clasped together, "you'll start tomorrow. We can move your stuff in tonight".

That's how she found herself in Boston's truck with Ruger and Cowboy following behind on their bikes. "Make sure you grab everything. We can make a couple of trips if we need to," the man offered as they pulled into the motel parking lot. Addie undid her seatbelt as they parked before climbing out of the truck.

She walked over to her door as the three men followed behind her. The metal key jiggled in the door as she unlocked it. With her shoulder, she shoved into the door.

It was an old, run-down motel even further out from the city, it would have easily taken her an hour and a half, if not longer, to walk to the bar. She didn't even know where the body shop or tattoo shop were located.

The doors were creaking and stuck. The guys hated that she had been staying here but were even more glad she was leaving with them.

They took in their surroundings. The room looked mostly untouched, with only a few personal items laid out. Addie grabbed her backpack and collected her toothbrush, hairbrush, makeup bag, and phone charger. In under five minutes, she was fully packed and ready to go.

She slung her bag over her right shoulder and turned to the three men. "I just need to drop the key off, and then I'm all packed and good to go," she smiled, swinging the key around on her finger.

"That's all you have?" Cowboy asked, "This is barely enough for more than two nights."

"I've always had to travel light," she shrugged as she placed the keys in the lockbox outside her door. The look of pity was missed by Addie, but the three men all wore one.

In her backpack was all she had. Her whole life was in there, and that didn't feel right. Boston gave the other two a look. A look that meant not to say anything else.

Climbing back into the truck, Addie placed her book bag between her feet. "Thank you again for everything," she smiled at Boston as the man drove. It was just them in the truck. Ruger and Cowboy were now moving ahead of them.

For some reason, Addie liked watching them on their bikes. It was cool. "I promise I'll give my first week's rent as soon as I make enough. If you need anything before then, I think I have a couple of twenties on me," she added.

Boston's teeth ground together. He needed to reign in his anger. He couldn't let it out in front of this sweet girl. She was too soft. "That's alright, Adelynne. First week's free. Call it a trial run to see if you can handle staying at the clubhouse".

_ell_

As Boston had called it, the clubhouse was where she spent the night once. Cowboy gave her a grand tour while Boston and Ruger walked off. She couldn't get a good read on the latter. He was gruff. Didn't talk much. He looked like he could kill someone if they looked at him the wrong way. She was sure he hated that they had brought her here, but she didn't bring it up.

"And this room is your room.." Cowboy explained as he opened the door near the end of the hall. It was right next to the room she had woken up in the night after being at the bar. "It used to be Dallas' when she still lived here. Anything she left you can use."

Addie's mouth dropped open as she took a look around the room. It was definitely Dallas' badass style here. Something the complete opposite of Addie's, but in a way, it felt cool to have a room like this.

The drapes were black, and the walls were painted a deep forest green. Everything about this room screamed dark and edgy. It starkly contrasted Addie's personality, but she loved it. She also loved the look of the plush bed in the middle. It looked a lot better than what she was used to.

"Thank you so much, Cowboy," Addie couldn't have been more thankful. "You can decorate as you please, paint the walls, change the curtains; we don't care."

"Ruger's room is next to yours. Mine is across from his, and Boston's is at the end. If you need anything, feel free to come to us".

# Chapter FOUR

**R**ock music pumped through the speakers as Addie scrubbed at the bar top with a rag. The sleeve of her yellow cardigan was becoming wet from the water and cleaner. She had worked several shifts at the bar and enjoyed meeting new people as they came in for a drink or two.

Boston would check in on her for the most part. He'd grab a drink, sometimes just stopping by for a quick chat with Patriot.

Addie didn't mind being around the man. Sure, he didn't speak much, mostly grunting in response. He acted like a caveman.

It made sense; most of the guys around here acted like that. The other half of them had tried hitting on Addie. They were all in a daze that someone so sweet and innocent was within their closed-off space.

From her time here, she had realized that the only people in this bar wore the same matching patch on their cuts. Dallas had explained about the club, and Addie didn't know if that made her more comfortable or nervous to be around so many of them.

The members she knew personally had been kind in their own way, but the ones she met at the bar seemed different. Boston had been sure to drill it into her head that not everyone was as nice as them. She needed to be aware of her surroundings and be suspicious of everyone.

"Can I get another beer, Lovey?" the caramel-eyed man asked with a smirk. He sat right in front of where Addie was cleaning. He'd been in almost every time she was working. He made the girl slightly uncomfortable but had never done anything to warrant those feelings. Yet, Boston's words hurled back at her. *Be suspicious.*

She looked at the bottle he held in his left hand before nodding. She reached into the fridge behind her, grabbing an iced cold beer for the man. She'd gotten quicker at opening the bottles with the bottle opener. It had taken her a few times to master it, broke a few bottles in the process.

"Here you are. It'll be another $4.50," she paused, waiting for the man to pay her. He placed a $5 bill in her hand, his touch lingering too long on her skin, "Keep the change."

She nearly rolled her eyes at his attempt at a tip. He always did this. She didn't mind small tips, she understood how tight money could be, but it was annoying to hear him brag about all the money he had, and he couldn't even tip her a full dollar.

"Congratulations on fifty more cents," Patriot chuckled lightly when Addie walked by him. She let out a huff of exasperation. She really disliked the man at the bar, but she knew he'd never try anything with Patriot keeping an eye on her. She felt safe working with a man as big and scary-looking as Patriot.

"Yeah, yeah, next time he's yours."

Boston had been acting weirdly since she started working here. He was overprotective one moment and then distant the next. She had stopped asking Patriot if the man was in.

"Prez said you could leave early today.' Patriot explained as Addie threw her rag into the wash bucket. "He's staying back, has a meeting or something."

Great, that meant that she needed to find her own way to the clubhouse. "Yeah, okay, thanks for letting me know."

It shouldn't bother her that the man had been quiet around her. Every time she caught him looking at her, he looked like his heart was breaking. She didn't understand. She had tried asking him a few times, but he'd shake his head and mumble the word 'nothing' under his breath.

Cowboy and Dallas were the two people she spoke with the most, the pair of siblings always telling her stories and keeping her company. It was a welcomed distraction. Don't get her wrong, she loved being around the guys, but they all hid their secrets, and she knew she wasn't privy to them.

Addie said her goodbyes to Patriot as she grabbed her back-pack before heading out the back door. She needed to throw the trash out before she left. The dumpster was only a few feet from the door, and it was still light out, the sun starting to set in the distance.

She couldn't wait to get home. Her feet were sore, and she stunk of beer. She had spilled a pint while cleaning, which had drenched her earlier in the day. The bar wasn't explicitly dirty, but she felt like grime was covering her skin. She needed a hot shower and then go to bed.

She was lost in her thoughts. She didn't even notice a man approach her. "Didn't even say goodbye?" a husky voice spoke, anger evident on their tongue. Addie flung around, her bag dropping onto the pavement.

Caramel eyes caught her own. Great. Not this guy.

She bent down to scoop her bag back into her arms. "I gotta go," she said calmly. Why was he cornering her in the back of the bar? *'Trust no one,'* Boston's voice repeated in her head. A shiver travelled down her spine at the thought. He could be trouble.

"No, you're not going anywhere," he spat back, "not until I get what I deserve. What you want too."

As he moved closer to Addie, she stepped further away. With each step she took back, he took two forward. It wasn't long until her back hit the metal of the dumpster. A gasp fell from her. She looked to her left and to her right. She had no escape.

Stupid. She was stupid. She wasn't supposed to take the trash out, that was Patriot's job, but she was trying to be nice, and it wasn't even dark out.

*Nothing bad is supposed to happen in the daylight.*

His left hand reached out to brush her cheek. His knuckles rubbed against the skin. "Are you scared of me?" he asked as Addie tensed up. "N-no," she stuttered out. Don't show him you're scared. Never show you're afraid.

"Oh, I think you are," he smirked. It wasn't a sexy one; more terrifying than anything. Evil. Evil lay deep within him. "I'm glad. You should be scared of me."

His head bent forward, his nose drifting across her neck. She stopped breathing. Her mind told her to play dead; he wanted a reaction from her. She wasn't going to give him the satisfaction of anything.

"You smell like strawberries and vanilla, so sweet." His lips ghosted over her sweet spot. She tried to push him away, but he only gripped her wrist. Tears stung at her eyes. The smell of stale cigarettes attacked her senses.

She was going to throw up. She knew she would if this continued. "Please, let me go," she asked weakly.

"You've been flirting with me every shift. I'm just giving you what you want. What you need," his voice was right against her ear. She could feel his hot breath on her.

"Let go," she grunted as she tried to kick at his shin. That resulted in him pushing her back into the dumpster harder.

"I don't want this!" her voice raised as a cry bubbled from her throat. This only spurred him on. Her scent was intoxicating, and he continued to kiss and lick at her neck. With her wrists in one hand, his other hand travelled between their bodies.

"Shit," Addie heard someone mumble before the caramel-eyed man was ripped off of her.

She barely realized that Patriot was holding her close as they watched Boston beat the man before them. "Don't you ever touch her again!" he growled, "she's already been claimed. She's mine."

Blood poured from the man's nose and busted lip. He fought back but was not quick enough to get many hits on Boston.

"If I see you near her again, I will kill you myself. No God will keep you safe from me. When you're praying, remember you're praying to me for mercy. You won't be saved. I'll send you straight to Hell".

The other man's blood covered the president's hands, but Addie didn't stop him from checking her over. His eyes glistened like he wanted to cry, but he was strong enough to mask his emotions after a moment.

"Let's get you home, Addie. Ruger will deal with Leon. He won't be a problem for you again."

Leon, so the man finally had a name.

Boston's arm wrapped around the girl's shoulder as he led her around the side of the building. He was tense. He was beyond being pissed off. Someone from his club thought he had the right to demand something from this girl, from his girl.

He knew Patriot would watch Leon while Ruger came to deal with him. He felt sickened that he hadn't protected Addie like he had promised. He should have protected her better. Protected them both better. But he was almost too late again.

# Chapter FIVE

S pending the day cooped up in the tattoo shop wasn't that bad. These days were nice and refreshing. Addie was allowed to sit behind the counter and read most of the day.

Sometimes she'd run down to one of the local food businesses and pick up lunch or dinner for those working in the shop that day, or she'd answer emails and the phone when it rang.

Ruger was stationed in the back corner. His room was mostly closed off by the half wall. He had more privacy due to him being the owner. Two other guys worked in the shop, one named Marco and the other named Wes. The two were brothers, mostly speaking Spanish amongst themselves.

Then there was Molly. She would come and go as she pleased. She was beautiful, her white blonde locks cascading down her back. She was good-looking too. Petite with big boobs. She also ignored everyone in the place besides her clients. She wasn't necessarily rude; she was just quiet.

Addie didn't mind. She would just read instead. She was grateful she always had a charger because her phone would die within the first half of her shift. With no one to talk to and her books to entertain herself, she was as content as possible.

Ruger's eyes would watch Addie anytime she moved around the shop. She could feel his stares. Since the incident at the bar, Boston, Cowboy, and Ruger had become more protective of her. She wasn't allowed to be in alleyways anymore and needed to text one of them whenever she went anywhere. She was starting to feel like she was suffocating.

She wasn't used to this. Dallas explained that's how they treated her too. She was becoming part of the family. She should feel grateful for it. She never had a family, and now the guys treated her like some kid sister. In a way, it felt nice, but she wasn't used to it.

"Hey, Mami," Marco called over to Addie. She looked up from her phone and turned to face the man. He was working on a client's leg tattoo. It was some badass design with skulls and roses, done in all black ink. "Can you do a food run? I won't be able to stop for a while."

It was nearing nine, and even Addie's stomach had started to growl an hour or two ago. "Yeah, I can grab something." She hated to admit that the man from the bar had made her a little more anxious about being out alone. The tattoo shop was in a small town outside of Austin, but she still felt uneasy. It didn't help that Boston didn't like the idea at all.

Ruger's eyes lifted from his own work. His jaw clenched as she grabbed her phone and some cash from the drawer for dinner. He watched as Addie checked in with Wes and Molly to see if they wanted anything before she approached him.

"Make sure you have your phone," he grumbled. He was tense, and even Addie could tell that something was up, but she knew not to question him. "I have it right here," Addie said with a wave of her hand, her phone gripped tightly. "Do you want anything for dinner?"

For a moment, all Ruger did was stare at the girl before him. "Do you have enough cash with you?" His teeth ground together as he started working on the man before him again. "Yes," he was frustrating some nights. Never answering questions, just supplying more. She'd just get him his regular, and he would have to deal with it.

With one last look at Ruger, Addie stuffed her phone into her pocket before walking to the front of the shop. The sun had already started to set. A cooler breeze in the air. Autumn was about to start, and the late Summer heat had nearly vanished.

It wasn't nearly as cold as some of the places she had lived growing up; the Summers here were hot. She had gotten so used to the warmer weather that she was spoiled with it. She was grateful for the cardigan she wore.

Their usual spot was a sub shop a few blocks down. The owner, Ronnie, was an older gentleman. He was always kind to Addie when she came in. He claimed she reminded him of his late wife, that her smile lit up his little shop. She would spend a long time in the shop talking with the man. His greying hair and wrinkles around his soft, brown eyes were a welcomed sight on her bad days.

"Adelynne, what are you doing out tonight?" Ronnie asked cheerfully as he noticed the girl walking in. She was usually joined by one of the grumbly men from the shop. It was only him to take care of customers this late at night. His staff were mostly students, and he didn't want them working too late.

"Hey Ronnie, just stopping by to pick up dinner for the crew." She leaned across the high counter, resting her arms in front of her. "The usual, please."

Addie had learned over the few weeks that Ronnie's wife had recently died of cancer. It was something the older man was struggling with. He threw himself into his work instead of allowing it to consume him. He claims that seeing everyone's smiling faces helped ease his pain.

Her phone buzzed in her pocket, but she ignored it. She was too busy catching up with Ronnie. "When again is your grandson coming back from college?" Ronnie loved to talk about his grandson, Zach, any chance he could bring him up. Addie was convinced the older man was trying to play matchmaker between them. She didn't mind too much as it made the man happy.

"He'll be home for Thanksgiving, so only in a few weeks will you get to meet him," his warm smile widened. "I think I'd like that," Addie replied happily.

She took the plastic bag of sandwiches from Ronnie before saying her goodbyes.

Her phone buzzed again as she turned to walk out the door. Ronnie stopped her as her hand reached the handle. "Tell that grumpy biker that he needs to keep a better eye on you. Someone may take you away before he realizes".

Addie just sent a smile his way before stepping out onto the sidewalk. She didn't know what Ronnie was getting at, and she wasn't too concerned.

When Addie made it back to the shop, Ruger looked pissed off. She handed Wes and Marco their sandwiches before travelling to Molly's station, leaving hers on the counter against the wall.

"My office, now," Ruger growled out as Addie approached him. Her eyebrows knit together in confusion. The man was normally rumbly and grumpy, but she didn't understand why he acted like this.

She huffed a sigh before storming off to Ruger's back office. She was just doing something nice, even grabbing food for Ruger. Did she take too much from their cash box? Was that why he looked ready to rip her head off? It was the normal, agreed-upon amount.

Ruger followed her into the room before slamming the door shut. Addie spun around to face him, her hands gripping the edge of the desk as her back hit the wood.

"You know the rules, Addie," his low voice spoke, "Do you intentionally break them? Are you stupid, or don't you realize the trouble you could get into?"

Addie gave him a dirty look. "I'm not stupid," she scoffed. Irritation was evident in her posture and voice. "What rule did I supposedly break?" Her arms crossed against her chest.

Ruger edged closer to the girl. "How many calls did you ignore when you left here?" Addie swallowed hard before she answered, noticing how dark Ruger's brown eyes had gotten. "Um... two?" she winced at the answer as it came out of her mouth.

"And how many should you have answered?"

"Both." she breathed out as Ruger stood directly before her. "What did we say would happen if you broke a rule?"

Addie gasped, "You can't be serious. I'm not a child." she glared at the man. A spanking. That was the punishment. She had thought they were kidding.

"We can do this the easy way or the hard way," Ruger supplied as a response. "Take your pick."

"I'm not letting you spank me!" she exclaimed.

"If you were mine, you'd already have a red hot ass for all the sass you've given me," he said with determination. "Chest on the desk. You don't want me to ask again."

She should tell him no. That he was out of his mind. That he was crossing the line. But she didn't. Why? Because the way he was staring at her was making her weak in the knees.

Addie leaned over the desk with another exasperated sigh, her chest pressing against the wood below her.

"I'll make it as quick as possible," he promised as his hand rubbed her lower back.

Addie muffled her cries with the sleeve of her cardigan as his hands struck her ass repeatedly through her jeans. "If you were mine, you wouldn't be privileged with the barrier of pants or panties."

This should be embarrassing, mortifying, really. Instead, it was a turn-on. This scene resembled one Addie had read in one of her romance novels. "Yes, Sir, I understand."

"Good, good, come here."

He held his arms out for Addie, pulling her against his chest. "I'm sorry I ignored your calls. I was just talking to Ronnie," she explained. That's when she remembered what the older man had said.

"He wanted me to tell you something. He said: Tell that grumpy biker that he needs to keep a better eye on you. Someone may take you away before he realizes."

"That old man needs to mind his own business. Come on, let's get you home. I'm sure you don't want to sit down right now," he smirked, "but you took it like a good girl."

There again, those feelings swirled within Addie. She was going to lose it because of these three protective men.

The shock was written across Boston and Cowboy's faces at what Ruger had just told them. "You spanked her?" Cowboy spluttered over his coffee the next morning. "She knew what would happen if she broke a rule," Ruger replied with a shrug.

Boston sipped on his coffee quietly as his eyebrows knit together in thought. He placed his mug down on the stone countertop. He was the most patient and level-headed of them all. "How did she react to it?" he asked thoughtfully.

"Pretty sure she soaked through her panties," Ruger smirked, "she cries pretty, by the way. So beautiful." The images flashing through his mind were sinful, and if he didn't divert his attention soon, he'd need a cold shower before work.

"I'll keep that in mind," Cowboy said as he rolled his eyes, "I better head out. She's probably waiting in the truck for me now".

She was. Addie was already seated inside the black truck. She was reading, and Cowboy knew she loved to read books on her phone. Sometimes he could hear her chatting with Dallas about pieces of her books. She'd get excited and blush while telling her friend about the men in the books. Romance shit.

Addie wasn't a morning person. Everyone around her in the morning could tell. It was best to leave her to her books until she had fully woken up and sunshine was back. Cowboy left her to her reading while he drove, drumming his fingers on the steering wheel along to the lightly playing music on the radio.

When they arrived at the bike shop, Dallas was already there opening up shop. The two siblings had opened the shop almost five years ago. Their parents had given them some money for Cowboy's 21st birthday, and he used it to set up shop at the farm. As their business grew, Dallas joined in to help her brother out.

Nearly five years later, they owned a small garage with a long list of clients. Many Rising Tide members got their bikes worked on by the Caville siblings. It was hard for those men to trust anyone with their bikes, but they felt better that it was their vice president and MC princess.

"Morning, Dal," Cowboy called out to his little sister as he slammed the driver's door shut. The echo of Addie's door closing was heard shortly after.

"Morning, Cowboy! Morning Ads".

Addie rushed her way from the truck to the shop to see her friend. Like a lost puppy seeing its owner again. "Morning, Dallas! Today is going to be a great day, I know it!" there the sunshine girl was, finally awake.

Cowboy let the two girls catch up on the latest gossip as he walked around, turning all the lights on. There were only enough room for four bikes inside the garage at a time. A small office was in the back corner next to the restroom. There was also a stock room that held miscellaneous parts.

It was small, but it was his, and he was proud of all he had accomplished.

Addie situated herself on the stool next to Dallas' workstation. The girl didn't have to do much at the body shop. She'd occasionally sign for packages when deliveries came in. She'd set customers up with appointments and handle payments. Besides that, she spent most of her days entertaining the youngest sibling.

Both Dallas and Cowboy enjoyed having Addie around. She brought a light to the shop, ensuring their days were always exciting. Cowboy always made sure to pay the girl well for her time, giving her more money for the least amount of work compared to Ruger and Boston.

Dallas was working on a bright red bike. Addie didn't know much about bikes, but this one was beautiful. This client wasn't a part of the club; she knew that by looking at the ride. MC members all had the same style and colour of bikes, all black. Dallas was fixing dents in the side of it and would then be repainting the motorcycle in the beautiful cherry paint to deal with the scratches.

The owner had been caught in a storm and lost control of her bike. Skidding across the wet asphalt left dents and grooves in the metal.

Addie looked over at Cowboy, hoping that the man was too distracted by his work to listen in on her confession. "One of them spanked me last night," she spewed out in a rush, the words garbling a bit.

Dallas' head whipped around, dropping the tool she held in her hand, the clank of metal hitting the concrete floor. "Which one? Boston?" The girl had noticed how protective of the girl her brother and his friends had gotten over the weeks. She wasn't sure what was happening between them all, but she enjoyed some juicy gossip.

"No, Ruger." A blush crept up Addie's neck, sinking into her cheeks. A gasp sounded from the girl beside Addie, "shut up!" she squealed. "Was it delicious? How are you sitting? That man is built.

I wouldn't be able to sit for a week if a man like that spanked me. What did you do?"

The questions came out rapidly, and all Addie could do was laugh. "I didn't answer his calls while grabbing dinner last night."

"And it was definitely better than I expected. I probably looked like a fool crying, but it was better than I had imagined. You and the books were right," she was now officially bright red like a lobster. She had enjoyed her spanking a little too much.

"What does this mean now?" she wondered out loud. She had no idea where this put her and Ruger's friendship. Something felt different now, like everything had shifted.

"It means my brother and Boston have stiff competition," the dark-haired girl said excitedly. This was every book girl's dream, having three men fighting over her. "I know I wasn't as cool about my brother liking you initially, but he needs to step up his game before he loses you to the man who barely talks."

Addie's eyes flicked over to Cowboy, watching his muscles flex as he worked on the bike before him. His sweat rolled over his shoulders, glistening. She'd be lucky to end up with any of them. They were all very attractive in their own ways. All extremely protective in a way that made Addie's thighs clench together. They were a dream.

"How am I supposed to choose one of them, Dallas? I don't want this to ruin a friendship". It was true. It was something Addie had been worrying herself over. "They're like brothers. I can't come between that".

"Well, you could cum between them, solve that issue," Dallas hit back fast, like the filter for her mouth had magically vanished for ten seconds. She had shocked herself by what she said, her eyes widening. "Let's pretend I didn't just talk about you cumming with my brother and his friends. That was weird".

Addie's laughter filled the garage. She swung her head back, nearly knocking herself off of the stool. Feeling this carefree for the first time in a while was good. Dallas made her feel that way. There was no judgment between the girls, and it's what Addie had always craved.

It was unfamiliar territory, having a friend like this. In some ways, they were as close as sisters. She didn't know what she had done to deserve this, but she never wanted to lose Dallas. She could never live without the spirited girl next to her. They were two peas in a pod.

Cowboy's eyes lingered on Addie as the girl laughed along to whatever his little sister had said. It was a nice change to hear genuine laughter and the happiness radiating off of someone like that. It warmed his heart.

"Okay, okay, it wasn't that funny," Dallas claimed with fake annoyance. She huffed, puffing her chest before pouting and returning to her work. Her back now facing Addie.

"Get back to work, you two, stop slacking," Cowboy hollered over to the two girls, pulling his earbud out as he did so, "we've got some money to earn today. Chop chop!".

Addie saluted the man before hopping off the stool and performing her normal activities. Starting with the inventory. How boring.

# Chapter SIX

E verything seemed to be going smoothly. She felt like she was finally doing something with her life. She was always working, but she was happy. She had spoken to Dallas and apologized for being such a shitty friend. They made up, and life was great.

Over the weeks, she had grown closer to Cowboy and Boston, and Dallas warned her that it probably wasn't a good idea to choose one. Cowboy and Boston were close, like brothers. Addie didn't want to be a cause for a fight. So she distanced herself whenever one of the men flirted with her or was just being nice.

It was a hard line to ride between being just friends and being something more. Even though she was happy, the nerves still ate at her. At least the days she worked at the tattoo shop with Ruger, she could breathe.

If Addie hadn't heard the man speak occasionally, she'd swear he was mute. Their drive to work was always quiet, as was the ride home. Whenever Addie was going to work with someone, they used Boston's truck. The man didn't mind. It seemed he had rules about someone riding on the back of one of his men's bikes or something. She felt that was a bit much, especially since Dallas sometimes rode on the back of Ghost's bike. But maybe that was different because she was Cowboy's sister.

Addie tugged at the end of her dress, pulling it back down over herself as she hopped off the stool set up by the front of the shop. She was wearing a brown chunky sweater under a brown plaid dress. On her feet were a pair of light brown boots. She had bought herself some more clothes as the weeks had gone on. She knew she'd need some warmer items before winter.

She was growing more and more tired as the night went on. It was just Ruger in at this point. The other artists had finished around ten. It was nearing midnight, and Ruger was still working on his client. A girl named Julie, Addie thought. Addie just knew she was being annoying, and her patience for the girl was wearing thin.

Her steamy romance book was put down as she shuffled around the studio. She was just getting to a good part of her book. She was feeling hot. All she could think about was the sexy man she worked for. Maybe it should be a turn off. A big no no even. But the idea of sleeping with her boss was hot; it was even more desirable that he was a biker too.

She watched as Julie flirted with Ruger. The man studied her thigh as he worked with precision. It had been a few hours, but the flirting was getting worse and worse. Addie couldn't stand it anymore.

Addie stood with her arms crossed as she glared at Ruger. His left hand was splayed on the girl's thigh as he worked on shading the piece. She was jealous. She shouldn't be, but she was.

Julie caught Addie's stare and scoffed. The girl rolled her eyes at Addie before placing her hand high on Ruger's thigh. She stared at Addie while she did it. Like she was staking her claim.

Ruger's eyes flicked up to Julie before turning to look where Julie was staring. He could see the flush of pink on Addie's cheeks, the way her chest heaved up and down as she tried to steady her breathing. Eyes flicking back to Julie.

Ruger slid his rolling chair back as he turned off the tattoo machine. "Alright, I think it's time to call it quits. Once this heals up in a few weeks, we'll have you come in and finish up with colour. We'll schedule your follow-up with Molly".

Molly was the wife of one of the club members. She was a badass tattoo artist and did excellent work. But she wasn't Ruger. Julie pouted at that. "Oh, I can't finish this with you?" she batted her eyelashes at him.

Ruger grunted, "I think it'd be best for Molly to finish this piece." He didn't leave it open for discussion; he was putting his foot down.

He cleaned Julie up and wrapped her new tattoo. He briefly reviewed the healing process and what to do before sending her on her way.

Addie had already gone back to her desk. She was embarrassed by how she acted. Ruger barely even looked at her. Why was she acting like this? Because she wanted more from the man.

After Ruger cleaned up, he stalked over to Addie. She was too into the sex scene in her book to notice he was standing right behind her. A scene between a boss and their employee played out, and Addie was turned on. His hot breath tickled her ear as he peered at her phone, reading the words.

"What's a good girl like you reading something so naughty?" he asked sincerely. His voice nearly made Addie moan. She rarely heard him speak, but it made her panties wet when he did.

She shuddered as she quickly flipped her phone. She placed it face down on the desk in front of her. "I don't know what you're talking about, Ruger." Addie played innocent. Her thighs rubbed together as she tried to subtly give herself some friction.

"Oh no?" he asked, his chest pressing against her back. "So you're telling me that your panties aren't dripping wet right now?" Addie gasped at his accusation. He wasn't wrong, but that's beside the point. "Soaked, picturing that scene between you and me?".

Her legs involuntarily spread a bit with his words. Like she was welcoming the rough man to touch her. "You want me to touch you. To feel how wet you truly are, hmm?" he asked as he pressed his lips to right under her ear.

Addie moaned lowly. She closed her eyes as Ruger slipped his right hand over Addie's breast. It snaked down her stomach before ending at the end of her shorter skirt. He waited a moment, watching her reaction. He'd pull away the moment she asked him to, but she didn't. She wouldn't.

His fingers dipped below her skirt, feeling her saturated cotton panties. "Aww baby, I'm sure you need to come. Your clit must be throbbing," the man muttered. Addie's breathy whimper was enough confirmation for the man. "What do you need?"

Addie's blush intensified. She couldn't possibly tell him. She looked back at him. A look of need was painted on her face. "Use your big girl words and tell me what you need, baby."

"You," she admitted, "I need you, Ruger."

"Stand up," Ruger ordered as he pulled his hand away. He gave Addie space to stand. Her face was bright red, and her eyes were glassy with need.

Ruger took a good look over her. She seemed to try to make herself smaller under his stare, which stoked the fire within him.

"Go lay down at my workstation. I'll be right there to take care of you". Addie's feet mindlessly led her to Ruger's station. He had already cleaned up before he had interrupted her reading. She settled down on the chair, laying back against the leather. She watched as Ruger locked the door and dimmed the lights.

Not many people were out at this time of night, but he didn't want anyone seeing what they were doing. Didn't want anyone else looking at this beautiful girl and how she'd cum for him. He bet she'd look so pretty as she cried out for him. Because of him. It made him hard to think about it.

"Good girl," he praised when he saw she had done as she was told. He adjusted the chair a bit to accommodate them both. His knees hit the wooden floor with a thud. "Spread your legs," he murmured against her thigh. He pushed her skirt up on her hips to get a good view of her light blue panties. They were plain, simple. He'd change that. Find her something that would make her feel like a goddess.

Her legs spread, and he ran both hands up the outside of her thighs. He hooked his fingers along the waistband of the panties, his eyes reaching hers. Searching for permission. She nodded her head quickly.

With a tug, Ruger pulled her panties down and off her legs. Her boots were still on. She felt a bit silly. The feelings didn't last long as Ruger's head bent down. His tongue ran up her slit as he got a good taste of her.

Addie's hands gripped the armrests on the chair as she bit down hard on her lip. "Don't you dare muffle yourself. I want to hear everything. Every breathy whimper, every whine, I want to hear you as you cry out for me when I make you see stars." Ruger had pulled away to glare up at Addie.

For someone who wasn't much of a talker, Ruger had a way with words. Without waiting much longer, he dipped back down to feast on Addie. His tongue swirled around her clit. Flicking his tongue with expertise. Addie couldn't help but moan for him. For the way his hunger for her led the way.

Rock music helped contain her every noise for just them to hear. When two fingers were pushed into her, Addie gasped. Her eyes rolled to the back of her head. She couldn't help letting her hands wander through Ruger's short hair.

Her hips moved on their own. She was both chasing the high but also pushing him away. It was intense.

Ruger pulled his fingers from Addie, using his hands to hold her legs down. He ignored his hair being tugged by the girl. It actually spurred him on. He was going to ruin her. Ruin her for anyone but them.

"Ruger, please," she begged. She didn't know if she was begging him to stop or never stop. He somehow delved in deeper, thrusting his tongue inside her as his nose rubbed at her clit. He hummed, and that's when Addie lost it. "Oh God, please..." she whined as her orgasm took over.

Her legs were shaking from the intensity. She's never felt like this before. Not a result she could ever possibly recreate on her own. She felt like she could float away.

Ruger's eyes were dark, lust filled, as he pulled away from her. His tongue licked along his bottom lip as he stared at Addie. "That was fucking hot," he growled. His hand slid behind Addie's head. He pulled her body close to his as he stood up to lean over her.

Their lips met, and it felt like electricity. Addie's plush lips melded with Ruger's rough ones. His kiss was dominating. The way he held her like she could never get away. Addie could taste herself on his tongue. She groaned into the heated kiss.

When Ruger pulled away, Addie gasped for air. Ruger's smirk intensified. His forehead pressed against hers as he stared into her eyes. It was like he was searching for something.

He must have found whatever he sought because he hummed and pulled away.

Addie watched as he walked away. He went into the bathroom. She could hear the tap running, and Ruger held a warm washcloth when he turned. Quietly he wiped Addie clean.

"You look worn out, baby," he said quietly as he ran his thumb over her puffy lips, his hand resting on her face, "let's get you home."

He hadn't given Addie her panties back. He liked knowing she wasn't wearing anything under her cute little dress. She couldn't believe how this night had turned out.

It was nearly two in the morning when they finally arrived at the clubhouse. Ruger was a gentleman and helped Addie out of the truck. His arm was tucked around her waist as he led them into the main part of the house. It was a weekday, so only the four of them spent the night. The only long-term residents were Addie, Boston, Ruger and Cowboy.

The lights were dimmed as Addie and Ruger stepped through the door. To the left was the large living room with three black leather couches. A tv hung above the fireplace. It was a simple space. Nothing like what Addie had expected from a bunch of bikers.

Cowboy was sitting on one couch with his phone in his hand while Boston watched the door intently. Addie tried to pull away from Ruger as she noticed the intense stare coming from Boston. The oldest man watched on as Ruger's grip tightened on Addie's hip. He wasn't letting her run.

Ruger nodded at Boston in greeting as Cowboy looked up at them. "How was your night, Honey?" Cowboy asked sweetly, "Ruger wasn't too rough on you, right?".

Addie's cheeks flushed as she recalled their steamy kiss at the shop. "I think she'd like it rough," Ruger mused, "wouldn't you, baby?". His voice was low, but he knew the two other men in the room had heard.

Her face turned towards the floor. He wasn't wrong. But she was embarrassed that the two other guys she had been interested in were sitting in front of them. Like they were waiting for her to answer.

"I don't think Addie here likes soft and sweet," Ruger pulled Addie's panties from his pocket, hanging them on his pointer finger. "She seemed to like it rough and dirty, according to the little books she reads at work."

"Who knew our sweet little thing could be so dirty," Cowboy chuckled. Addie tried to reach out for her panties, her face bright red. She couldn't believe what he was doing. Parading around like he won a prize.

"Come here, Adelynne," Boston demanded. The way he commanded her, he meant business. Ruger's hold on her lessened as he let her go over to the older man. Her feet stopped in front of Boston's. "Sit," was his next order. Something was swirling in his eyes. Lust and maybe a bit of need.

She tried to sit on the couch beside him, but he didn't allow that. He pulled her onto his lap. Her knees were on either side as she straddled him.

She could feel herself rub against the fabric of his jeans. An unwanted mew fell from her lips from the feeling. "Not yet, Angel. We need to talk first". She didn't like the sounds of that.

"What you did with Ruger wasn't wrong," Boston explained as he brushed her hair back, "but we need to talk about it. The four of us".

"If you want to be with me, Baby, you need to be okay with being with them too," Ruger said quietly as he knelt on the ground behind her, "the three of us are a package deal. You can't just choose one".

Did she just hear that right? Maybe it was just that she was so overtired that she was misunderstanding. Boston lifted Addie's chin to look her in the eyes. "You don't have to decide tonight. You can sleep on it. Take your time because once we have you, we aren't letting you go".

"You all want me?" she didn't believe that. Those three men were fine as wine. They couldn't possibly all want her.

"I kicked out a paying client and told her I'd schedule her for a follow-up with a different artist because you were jealous. That should have proven to you that I wanted you," Ruger didn't mean for the words to come out so rough. He felt a little bad when Addie shivered as he spoke.

"We didn't want to push you. It's a lot to take in, Honey," Cowboy piped up. He moved to stand behind the couch to see Addie's face. She was surrounded by these men. These dark, scary, big men. She should have been scared or a little nervous, but she wasn't. She felt safe and protected.

"We've wanted you from the moment you walked into the bar the first night. You were already ours. You just didn't know it yet," Boston smiled warmly, "if you'll have us. If you don't, we'll find you employment elsewhere. We'll give you cash to get your place. We just can't keep pretending that we don't want you".

"I'm yours," she replied quietly, "I don't need time to think about it. I know what I want, and it's the three of you".

Boston tilted Addie's chin up before closing the gap between their lips. His kiss wasn't like Ruger's; it was dominant yet tender.

Addie fisted Boston's shirt as she melted into the kiss. She felt like a fire was being lit between them. The kiss was intense, and she kept chasing the high. She ground down on his lap as they kissed.

Boston grew harder beneath her as Addie moved her hips. His right hand made its way up her back and to the back of her head. He gripped her hair in his hand, tugging back slightly to pull her away so he could kiss her jaw and down her neck.

Addie gasped as he tugged her away. Her mouth fell open. Her glassy eyes shot past Boston's head to where Cowboy stood watching. She tried to find friction to get herself off, even though she knew she may be making a fool of herself.

As her moans and whines grew louder, her breathing becoming panting, she was pulled off Boston's lap. The older man had let her go. She was held up against Ruger's chest. Her feet fell to the floor. She didn't even care that her skirt was still hiked up. The fabric barely kept her covered at this point.

Cowboy moved around the couch to be right in front of Addie. "Do you want to go to bed?" he asked cautiously. She could cry with how frustrated she was getting. Why did Boston stop? Why did Ruger pull her off of Boston? She wasn't understanding.

"We need to know if you can take us tonight." To the guys, this would officially make her theirs, and they would never let her get away. This was her last chance to turn away.

Addie tried to grab Cowboy's face, wanting to kiss him, but Ruger held her arms back. "Words, baby."

"Take me, please," her eyes flicked between Boston and Cowboy.

Cowboy nodded before turning. Ruger helped steady Addie before the four of them went upstairs. She was so wet. She could feel the slick on her thighs as they rubbed together.

The four found themselves in Boston's bedroom. With three pairs of hands on her body, Addie found herself stripped of her remaining clothing quickly.

Cowboy's lips found Addie's, pulling her in deeply. Hands ran down her side and settled on her hips while someone else's hands cupped her breasts. Her nipples were hard as stones as they were flicked and twisted.

When she gasped at the feeling, Cowboy slipped his tongue between her lips.

Kisses were placed softly on her jaw while someone nibbled and sucked on the other side of her neck. The sparks were intense. Wave after wave of stimulation was sent to her clit.

One of the hands playing with her nipples snaked down her stomach. She spread her legs as the hand cupped her. A finger slid between her folds.

"Fuck," Boston groaned, "you're soaked, Adelynne. So wet for us".

Addie moaned as his finger circled her clit. It wasn't enough. "On the bed, hands and knees, Baby," Ruger ordered when Cowboy had pulled away. You did not have to ask her twice.

She didn't know who had done it, but a hand was placed between her shoulder blades, pushing her down into the position they wanted her in. Her chest was pressed against the mattress, her ass in the air. Someone had tapped her legs, telling her to spread. She was all on display for the three hungry men to see.

"How do you want this, sweetie?" Cowboy asked from some-where behind her.

"We're all clean. Are you on birth control or something?" Boston asked as he reached down to rub her clit.

"You can go bare; I'm clean," she whined as she ground down on Boston's hand. His fingers trailed to her entrance before pushing two fingers in. She was incredibly tight, and Boston found himself cursing under his breath. "We'll start gently," Boston promised.

Addie nodded her head as quiet moans poured from her lips. When Boston knew she was wet enough, he pulled his fingers out of Addie, licking them. Her juices tasted better than he imagined. He knew he'd never get enough of her taste.

Cowboy was the most gentle of the three, so he went first. His clothes were thrown in a pile at the end of the bed. His hard cock hit his stomach as he took in the sight before him.

Addie was beautiful. He couldn't believe he was going to expe-rience the feel of her sweet pussy first.

"I'll go slow. Let you adjust," he murmured as he slipped his tip between her folds.

"You're so tight, fuck," Cowboy groaned as he slipped inside her. He took his time, allowing Addie to get used to his size. His head shot to look at the roof. He swore he'd bust if she so much as coughed.

"Move, move," she begged. Who was he to tell this woman no? His hips snapped forward, making her take him all the way. Her body thrust forward as she gasped. His thrusts were slow. Deliciously slow. Each drag of his cock made her want to beg for more.

"Oh yes!" Addie mewed, "Oh God!"

Cowboy's motivation was to make this gorgeous girl come undone on his cock. He lazily rubbed at her clit while his hips slowly thrust into her. It wasn't long before she came with a moan of his name. The feeling of her constricting around his cock set Cowboy off. His own orgasm rocked his world.

He placed a kiss between her shoulder blades before slowly slipping out of her. Boston quickly took his place. He'd already stripped down. His red cock leaking precum. He was so painfully hard from just hearing Addie's lovely moans.

"On your back, Adelynne," Boston ordered. It was like a switch had flipped. She immediately responded to his demand, rolling onto her back. It was then she noticed that Boston's long red hair wasn't in the usual bun he had it in. Right now, it was left down and cascaded down his chest.

Addie realized how vulnerable she was, Cowboy's cum leaking from her, and she was entirely on display. She hurried to cover her boobs. Boston gripped her wrists in one hand, pinning them to the bed above her head.

"Boys, we seem to have a goddess in our bed," Boston couldn't believe how beautiful the girl looked before him.

Sex with Boston was different compared to Cowboy; he was more dominant. His hold was tighter, his moans louder, but the pleasure was indescribable. "Come on, Adelynne, cum for me," he ordered. She didn't know if she had it in her. But the way he commanded her body had her reaching her peak again. She was sure the sheets were soaked at this point. Even more when Boston pulled out after reaching his climax.

From what she could tell, Ruger was the biggest of them all. "Fuck, Baby. You're looking at me like I'm about to break you," he chuckled, a smirk widening, "I'm going to break you. Ruin you. For anyone but us." It was a promise.

Before Addie could reply, Ruger had her flipped onto her side. Her back to his chest. He was rougher than the other two men. He was quick to impale her on his cock.

A cry fell from her lips as his hips roughly jutted upwards. His fist found hair wrapped around itself, pulling her head back to get a good angle at her neck.

He could see it was already littered with bites he had left previously. He was marking her as his own. "Going to make you feel me for days," another promise.

"You're so fucking tight, even after being ruined by two other cocks. You took them like a good girl, didn't you?"

"Yes!" she shouted as his thrusts sped up. "My good girl, hmm?" he kissed below her ear. "Letting me eat her out at work."

"Such a dirty girl reading her dirty little books while looking like an innocent treat."

Addie was clenching down on him so tightly. With every sentence, she was nearing another release. "You're so filled with our cum, Baby. I bet you can take another load. Are you going to be a good girl and cum for me?".

"I can't," Addie shook her head before feeling her hair tugged again, in a tighter grip than before.

"Tsk tsk, Baby. Isn't this what you wanted? Wanted to feel so full of us? If you want my cum, you'll do as I say".

His hand left her hair and moved around to her throat. His grip tightened as he approached his orgasm. "You'll take what you can get from us, Baby. And you will reward me with what you have to offer."

With a cry, a powerful orgasm ripped through Addie. She was blindsided by it. Spots of black appeared in her vision. She was flipped onto her front as Ruger grabbed her hips roughly. He entered her again. Fucking her hard and deep, all Addie could do was whine into the mattress. Her brain was a pile of mush.

His hips stuttered as ropes of cum filled Addie. "Such a good girl doing as she's told," he growled as he pulled out.

She was utterly spent. She barely remembered someone cleaning her with a warm washcloth. Someone had also made her drink some water. All she wanted was to sleep and enjoy the warmth her brain was giving her. She was riding a high.

# Chapter SEVEN

When morning came, Addie found herself pressed against someone's hard body. She could feel the rough tip of their finger dragging across the skin on her wrist. They were being as gentle as they could not to wake her up.

Her head was pressed against their chest, tucked below their chin. When she opened her eyes slowly, she recognized some of their tattoos. Ruger. She was cuddled up to Ruger. The scary, grumpy-pants of a man. Hers.

Memories from the night before flooded through her. She could feel the delicious ache in her body from how those three men claimed her as theirs. She was theirs.

She had never felt safer in her life than around those three men. She knew they'd give anything to make her happy, to keep her safe.

Ruger's finger continued to drag across her skin. Across her scars. The very scars she had always kept hidden except last night. Last night everything was on display.

"Why did you do this to yourself?" was the first thing Ruger asked. He knew she was awake. He could tell by the pattern of her breathing. "I don't know. It helped," Addie shrugged. She didn't know why.

Ruger hummed. It was as if he understood. But how could he? Her answer was ridiculous. How did hurting herself help? It didn't. It just added to the chaos her demons caused.

"If I was angry, I took it out on myself. When I was sad; I'd do it because it made me feel better... There were things that made me feel like I was nothing, so I'd prove it to myself, I guess".

The room was silent at her confession. Addie was nervous that he'd see how broken she was and back out of whatever they had going on.

She focused on the warmth of the sunlight peaking through the curtains. Focusing on anything else as she pretended she wasn't about to lose everything all over again. They'd call her a freak. They'd leave her. It would only further prove that she was worth nothing.

"I drank to deal with my pain," Ruger admitted after a few minutes. His face was turned up towards the ceiling. His left hand rubbed Addie's back through the thin sheet covering her body.

"It wasn't pretty, but I didn't think I had a problem."

She was surprised he was opening up to her. She figured he only spoke with people he trusted.

"I didn't think I needed any help. I was fine on my own. Boston and Cowboy helped me, though. In more ways than they know".

Ruger was silent for another moment. It was hard for him to be open, to be vulnerable. He wasn't used to this, but he wanted Addie to know.

"I was a marine," he started, "I was a sergeant. Had a whole squad that was under me. That relied on me. I did two tours and was away from home for years".

Addie had noticed the dog tags he always seemed to wear but never thought it was the right time to bring them up.

"I enlisted when I was 18. I was freshly graduated and officially on my own for the first time in my life".

"My father thought I could do with some kind of structure in my life. Something to keep me grounded after we lost my mom and little sister."

She could feel the pain lacing his words. "And it worked. I learned how to contain my anger and channel it in different ways."

"When I lost my whole squad and nearly lost my arm, all that pent-up rage came back to the surface. My father stopped visiting. I lost everyone I had cared about. I was turning to whiskey to numb myself. I didn't realize how deeply I was drowning until Cowboy and Boston pulled me above water".

Addie had noticed the scars on Ruger's right shoulder. Most of it was still dark pink. She knew whatever had happened must have been painful to live through.

"I almost fully lost my arm. I've had multiple surgeries and spent two years rehabbing my arm to the point I could write again."

Her delicate fingers traced his scar carefully. The raised scar tissue brought up tears. She felt for the man she was curled up to. He lost everyone and nearly lost a part of himself.

"Boston took care of me for a few months. He let me stay here if I agreed to get my drinking under control. I barely drink now; I don't want to lose that control again".

"Cowboy helped me financially. Because of him, I have a shop. They both knew I could recover from this and do something positive with my life. They're like brothers to me. I'd do anything for them. And now I'd do anything for you because you're ours".

They laid there quietly. Ruger's hand was still rubbing at her back. "Why'd you come here, Addie?"

It was a question she had been hoping to avoid. "Dallas told us it seemed like you were running from something. By the looks of what you had with you at the motel, I agree. So what's your story?"

She could choose to lie. It's not like they could find much from a background check. Did she want to start this relationship out on a lie? No.

"I was about to age out of the system," she mumbled quietly, "I couldn't sit around and wait much longer. I needed out".

Ruger's hand stopped, floating above her back now. His eyebrows knit together. "You're not eighteen?" He was fucked. So fucked. Everything they had done the night before. Everything he had wanted to do to her.

"There's an extended program. I'm twenty. Well, almost twenty-one." The breath Ruger had been holding was released. It could have been worse, could have been seventeen. "Thank God," he sounded relieved.

"But wait, your ID says twenty-four?"

"You looked at my ID?" she questioned, "is that how Boston knew my name was Adelynne?" It made sense that they must have looked at her ID at some point or that Dallas had told them her first name.

"Cowboy wanted to know who was hanging around his sister. Anyway, back to your story".

"My last foster home was probably the worst out of them all. I did what I could to save money. I did odd jobs here and there. Mow the lawn, weed someone's garden. Anything I could do for those in the neighbourhood."

"None of them were ever good-paying jobs. They sucked, honestly. But I'd make a couple of dollars here and there. I lived in that home for about six years. I moved in just after my fourteenth birthday. In that time, I had managed to save a couple of grand. All cash".

"I know it's not a good idea to have cash like that lying around, but what was I to do? I was just a child. I couldn't even open a bank account on my own," Addie sighed as she continued.

"When the husband would get drunk, he'd break into my room. Find any cash he could and use it to buy more booze."

She didn't add anything more, allowing the silence to cover them again.

Ruger knew there was more to her story. He could tell she was choosing her words carefully, trying to hold bits and pieces back. He knew she must have gone through something bad; she just wasn't ready to discuss it. He'd help her. As Boston and Cowboy had done for him, he'd help her with her own demons.

Though their relationship was still fresh, Addie had agreed to meet Cowboy's family. Dallas had been the first to know about their relationship, and the girl was a little surprised but supportive of the four of them. Winning over Mom and Dad? That scared her.

The four were going to spend the weekend at Cowboy's family farm. Once a month, he'd make the drive out to see his parents. He'd help around on the farm with any project they'd be up to. Boston and Ruger would go when they could to help out.

Cowboy's parents were getting older and could no longer do everything independently like they used to. The man felt it was his duty to care for the people who raised him, who took in his two best friends and treated them as their sons.

"They're going to hate me," Addie mumbled for the third time that day. The air had a slight chill to it today. The sun was high in the sky, and if it weren't for the slight breeze, Addie would have sworn it was still summertime.

Her outfit consisted of a cream, chunky knit sweater dress that came right above her knees. On her feet were a pair of reddish-brown cowboy boots. Her outfit was Cowboy's pick. He wanted her to be comfy but also prepared for being on the farm. Her canvas shoes just wouldn't cut it.

The drive wasn't too long. The farm was only 30 minutes from the clubhouse in a neighbouring town. Boston decided to drive; it was his truck. Ruger and Cowboy crowded on either side of Addie in the back seat. Did they need to be there? No. But something was going on between the two of them, and Addie didn't know what.

The tinted windows made it dark in the back of the truck. They were hidden from the outside world.

Ruger's palm slid up Addie's right thigh. At first, she thought nothing of it. She knew the quiet man loved touching her. Any moment he could, he would. Like he never wanted her to slip from his grasp.

She knew he was up to something when his hand continued to ride higher, slipping under the hem of her dress. A soft gasp fell between them as she looked wide-eyed at the man.

Boston's eyes flicked up to the rearview mirror. He knew what Ruger and Cowboy had planned. His eyes lingered momentarily before returning to the country roads before him.

"Relax, Honey," Cowboy gently ordered, "spread your legs. Let Ruger in". Addie did as she was told, spreading her legs as far as they'd go. Her thighs were now pressed against Cowboy and Ruger.

Ruger's rough fingertips ran across the front of her panties. The gentlest of touches started a fire within Addie. He could feel the moisture bleeding through the fabric. Knowing his baby was enjoying the idea of what they were about to do.

Cowboy's right hand followed under her dress. His fingers hooked into the band of her panties, tugging them down. Addie had to lift herself for him to move them to her knees.

Ruger took that moment to run his finger between her folds. His finger circled her clit before he pinched at it. Addie let out a hiss, mostly of pleasure, at what Ruger had done.

"We've got about twenty minutes, Cowboy. How many do you think we can get out of her?" Ruger asked while he continued to flick, pinch and rub at her clit.

"Oh, at least three," the bearded man nodded. "You're insane," Addie shook her head.

"Hush, Addie, the men are talking," Ruger tutted. She wanted to retaliate but felt Cowboy's fingers slip beside Ruger. A moan sprang through her chest as her men took care of her.

Her mind finally drifted away from her worries. All she could think about was the hands on her. The fingers inside her. She didn't know if Ruger or Cowboy had slipped two fingers deep inside her. Someone still rubbing at her clit.

"You're so wet, baby," Ruger growled. She could hear how wet she was. A whimper came as she felt the other hand insert a finger. They were stretching her.

"Do you think we'd break her if we took her at the same time?" Cowboy mused. He watched as Addie's head found a home in Ruger's throat. The double attack on her had her giving up. They were going to take her, and she wouldn't stop them. She wanted this.

"She can barely take one of our cocks. Hell, she's squeezing the life out of our fingers right now," Ruger said through gritted teeth, "imagine how tight she'd be if we had our way with her."

Addie gripped onto Ruger's left arm. Crying out, she felt the building of her orgasm. "She's going to ruin your poor seats, Bos. She's soaked."

They were talking like she wasn't even there. Instead of being upset, it spurred her on more.

Boston's fingers dug into the steering wheel. Turning white as his grip tightened. He didn't know why he had agreed to this. He was so hard in his jeans that it hurt. "Don't care about the seats, Cowboy." He didn't care about the seats.

"Please, please, please," Addie begged. Her mouth was kissing and biting down on Ruger's shoulder. "Cum, Baby," he ordered.

It was like she needed him to tell her body what to do. She felt him growl as she reached her release, squirting against their hands.

"Oh fuck me, that was hot," Cowboy said in shock. Pulling his slick-covered hand away from Addie's trembling body. "She covered us!"

"You did so well, such a good girl," Ruger said quietly as he grabbed a t-shirt Boston had left in the back when he went for a run earlier in the day. He gently cleaned her up, the fabric causing her to let out a hiss at the contact. She was sensitive.

When she thought they were done, she was dead wrong. Cowboy lazily played with her. Claiming an orgasm for himself before Ruger worked her up to a third. She was so wet and needy when they pulled into the farm's long driveway.

The rocks that formed the roadway crunched under the tires of the truck. "Doesn't look like they've made it back from the stores yet," Boston announced as they parked next to the little farmhouse.

The farm was situated along the tree line. A big barn in the back with a wild garden filled with any vegetable you could imagine. Cowboy's mom loved that garden. It was her pride and joy.

Along the tree line sat the large barn. It mostly held a few horses and farm equipment. The red-painted barn was very stereotypical looking, but Addie loved it.

She could finally take in her surroundings when her boots hit the rocks. She could see that there was also a large pond with two ducks swimming in it to the left of the house.

It felt very calming, safe even.

That was until Cowboy pulled her close by the waist, his lips pressing against her neck. "You're going to run, Honey, you're going to run and not look back. If we find you and catch you, we get to keep you forever".

A shiver of excitement ran through her at the thought of being caught. She wasn't scared to be stuck with them. She nodded her head, not yet trusting her words.

"Good, you get a minute for a head start. Better find a good hiding spot. We know this farm like the back of our hands," he added.

She looked around at her men's faces. A look of determination on each of them. The thrill of running from these hungry wolves sent her feet running. With a laugh, she took off.

Her head whipped around. Where could she hide? They had an advantage over her. They knew this place. She barely got a look at it. Her best bet was the woods. They couldn't know the woods that well.

She hoped.

Her boots pelted the ground as she neared the tree line. She knew she didn't have enough time to turn around and hide. She continued into the woods. She had to be careful in here, watch where she was going. She'd rather not make it easy by twisting an ankle on a tree root.

She could hear them call out from by the truck. They were coming. Excitement ran through her. This shouldn't get her going, but she was so hot for this. A little game of cat and mouse.

It wasn't long before she got lost in the woods. It may have been less than five minutes, but with all the turns she had made, she was a goner. She could hear Cowboy and Boston calling out for her. Taunting her.

A hand clamped over her mouth before she could scream. She was pushed up against a nearby tree. "I told you, you weren't getting away from me." Her shoulders sagged in relief. Ruger.

Of course, the ex-marine would find her first. It was in his blood, like some kind of hound dog.

His hand moved from her mouth, knowing she wouldn't try and scream at this point. She was a good girl. He knew she'd take him as he pleased.

His hands pulled her white cotton panties down to her knees, seeing they were coated in her slick. She was always wet for them. It was bad. Or good, depending on who you asked.

"Spread your legs, Baby, let me in," Ruger urged as the tip of his cock rubbed against her slit. She couldn't believe they were doing this. They were outside. Sure, they were surrounded by woods, but what if someone other than her men found her like this?

Addie whined as her face was pressed against the bark of the tree. Ruger's hips hit the back of her thighs as he sheathed himself inside her. She tried to muffle her moans. She bit her bottom lip to try and keep quiet.

"None of that," Ruger growled, pulling her bottom lip from between her teeth, "I want them to hear how good I fuck you."

Her little whimpers turned into full-on moans as he changed their position slightly. He was reaching deeper than Addie had imagined could be reached. Every time he pulled out and thrust back in, he rubbed against a spot driving her nuts.

She panted as his right hand wrapped around her throat. Gurgles were let out. From where her head was turned, she could see Cowboy enter her line of vision. He leaned up against a neighbouring tree.

"Are you going to be good and milk me of my cum?" Ruger groaned in her ear. Her sweet pussy clenched down on his throbbing cock. She was going to do whatever he asked of her. He knew it, and so did she.

She could feel the moment he reached his release. Hot spurts of cum lining her cervix. "Fuck, Baby, you're perfect," he admitted as he fucked her to her release.

Cowboy pulled her away from the tree, pulling her against his chest. Boston slid in front of her. Before she realized what they were doing, Cowboy's dick pressed against her opening. "What are you doing?" Addie asked, confused. Her head whipped around to find Ruger, where he was now standing beside the three of them.

A moan broke through as she felt Boston's fingers slip into her beside Cowboy's length. Ruger watched on with darkened eyes. He knew she could handle it. But he was watching her for her safety.

"We're going to fuck you, Adelynne," Boston said as if it was obvious. "Together?" she gasped. There was no way they'd both fit. "Together," Boston nodded.

The burning she felt as Boston's fingers thrust into her next to Cowboy had her rolling her eyes into the back of her head. "She's as ready as she's going to get," she heard Boston say, "is she okay to continue?".

Ruger nodded his head. She would be okay. "Tell them if you want them to stop," he explained to Addie. The guys had talked about this as they had watched her run away. Ruger had the most control when it came to this. He would make sure she was okay through her first time like this.

Cowboy and Boston were known for threesomes back in the day, but they had never cared so much about the girl they were with until Addie.

Addie cried out as Boston inched in beside Cowboy. Her legs spread wider to accommodate them. Her head laid back against Cowboy's chest. Her mouth opened as light pants, and whines fell from her lips.

"I'm not going to last long," Cowboy muttered under his breath, "didn't think she could feel this tight, fuck."

"You're doing so good, Baby," Ruger encouraged as his hand cupped her face softly, "taking them like a champ."

It wasn't long before Boston and Cowboy reached their release, and Addie followed suit.

Cowboy couldn't believe this girl was theirs. He couldn't wait to introduce her to his parents. Maybe they shouldn't have fucked her into oblivion, but now her mind was no longer focused on her anxiety.

She knew she'd be feeling what they had done in the woods for a while. She felt sore, and yet, she also felt so peaceful. Cowboy helped her pick the leaves and bark from her hair.

"You don't need to be nervous. They're going to love you," he promised as he held her close as they walked towards the house. Ruger and Boston were only a couple of paces behind.

The four toed off their boots, settling them on a tray by the front door. They could hear a couple laughing as pots and pans banged around. She wanted to be sick. She couldn't do this.

"Ma! Pa!" Cowboy greeted them like a little boy. It was obvious he was excited to see his parents. Addie stayed tucked behind the three men. She was debating making a run for it, but she saw the look Ruger was throwing her. She'd barely make it out the door before he caught her again.

"Rueben!" an older lady called back. From what Addie could tell, she was a petite woman, similar in size and shape to Dallas. Her greying hair was thrown up in a claw clip to keep it out of her face. She wore dark denim jeans and a faded black T-shirt. Her rosy cheeks and dimples were displayed as she smiled at her son.

"Lyle, Judas, come in. Come sit," she fussed over Boston and Ruger. Rushing around the table, she placed a pot on a trivet. A man was already seated at the end of the table. His jet-black hair was cut short. He wore jeans and a red and black plaid flannel. He looked like Cowboy, just a bit older and without a beard.

"Going to need an extra setting, Ma," Cowboy smiled at his mother as Ruger and Boston took a seat. The youngest man moved around the kitchen, gathering an extra plate setting for Addie.

"Is Allison coming for dinner tonight?" she asked before noticing Addie standing awkwardly in the doorway. "Oh, you brought a friend?" she asked excitedly, "come sit, sweetie."

Cowboy pulled out a chair for Addie beside his own. Ruger and Boston were seated across from them, with Cowboy's parents on either end.

Addie graciously thanked Cowboy before sitting down. "I hope you don't mind me interrupting your dinner," she started as she looked at both ends of the table. Cowboy's hand reached for hers, giving it a slight squeeze. She'd be okay.

"It's never an interruption. Any friend of Reuben or Allison will always have a place here with us." His mother was warm. Welcoming. She was thankful.

"What's your name?" Cowboy's dad asked kindly as he helped serve out dinner. He passed the bowls around the table. Some kind of beef stew, Addie thought.

"My name's Adelynne, but most people call me Addie," she smiled as Cowboy handed her a bowl of stew. He helped her settle it on her placemat to not burn her hands.

"Beautiful name for a beautiful girl. I'm Pam. And my husband is Richard." Pam introduced. "So, how did you meet our boys?" Richard asked. She was momentarily confused, "Lyle and Judas were essentially adopted by my wife and me."

"Oh, um, I met Dal... umm, Allison, when I first moved to town. I work for the guys now," Addie explained. Cowboy coughed a bit before looking down at Addie. "She's also my girlfriend," Cowboy spoke up. Addie's eyes flicked to Boston and Ruger.

"Let me rephrase, our girlfriend. She's ours."

A spoon clattering against a bowl made Addie want to run from the table. Run far away and hide. Silence spread across the table, and Addie played with her food. Swirling her spoon in her bowl, not knowing what to say or who to look at. Her appetite was long gone now.

Richard cleared his throat, directing the attention to himself. "If this makes you happy, Reuben, your mother and I support you."

"I'm sorry if I made you uncomfortable, Addie," Pam said with a warm smile, "that kind of relationship is not one we're used to. But, if you and the boys make our baby boy happy, then so be it. Doesn't matter if it's what others consider normal. Welcome to the family".

～ﾚﾚﾚ～

Throughout dinner, Cowboy's parents asked Addie all about herself. They learned that her favourite flowers were sunflowers. Her favourite colour was yellow, and she loved cats. They had informed her they had a barn cat with kittens a month ago.

That's how the four found themselves in the barn, hunting down kittens. "Baby, what will you do once you catch one?" Ruger asked as he looked behind a couple of hay bales. "Cuddle it, duh," she sassily replied as if it was an obvious answer.

# Chapter EIGHT

Addie never had her scars out in the open. Not because she was embarrassed by them but because of how angry she got when she saw them. Angry at herself for what she had done to her skin. Mad at the situations she was put in. But most of all, she was angry about all of the abuse and neglect she faced as a child.

Today was different. Today was her first day of healing. She was finally getting a fresh start. Ruger had opened the shop up to her on a Monday. It was just the two of them. Boston and Cowboy knew this may be best. If anyone could get her to open up, to spread herself open, allow him to see her every scar, it would be Ruger.

The two were close. They all had different relationships with Addie. Each gave her a piece of themselves that she needed. Boston understood what being in the foster care system was like. He knew what it was like to never know who your parents were.

Cowboy was good at comforting. Whenever Addie had night-mares or there were bad storms, Cowboy would be there to protect her. He'd whisper sweet nothings until Addie lulled herself to sleep. He'd hold her close to his chest.

Then there was Ruger. The normally cold and closed-off man. He was there for her to talk to about anything. He was a great listener. Addie could go on and on about her books or a tv show she was watching. He may not always respond, but she knew he was listening, taking everything in.

He showed her his darkness; in turn, his ray of sunshine showed her own. The moment he saw her physical and mental scars, he pledged to never allow her to hurt again.

His tattoo station smelt of cleaner. It was a welcoming scent to Addie. The scent grounded her. The scars on her thighs were light enough that few noticed, but the ones on her arms were still raised. Some were a deep pink, while others were turning an ivory colour. They all varied in age, Ruger had guessed.

The man helped settle Addie into the chair before sitting on his stool. Her eyes roamed over the little pots of coloured ink. She wasn't scared in the slightest. She knew Ruger would never hurt her. She also knew it couldn't be worse than what she had already done to herself.

"I want you to talk about it. Get it all out," Ruger explained as he slipped the black vinyl gloves on his large hands. He snapped them in place. "This is part of your healing. What you say here, to me, won't be repeated unless I deem it necessary". His eyes met

Addie's. Honesty was what she read from his eyes. She knew she could trust him. That's why she was here.

"Okay," she knew she needed to do this. She didn't want to carry this with her forever. She wanted to breathe one day. She needed to heal.

Ruger prepped Addie's skin on her forearm. Gently he laid the stencil down, aligning it perfectly before pressing it into her skin. Peeling the paper away, he looked at Addie as he lifted her arm. She could see that most of her scars were covered by the stencil. "Anything that's not covered by the stencil can be shaded over," he explained, "you may still be able to see some of the scars due to texture, but this will grant you freedom from your past."

This wasn't his first rodeo when it came to covering scars. He hated every session. Not because it made him uncomfortable but because he could see how much pain a person had been in to do that to themselves.

It was harder to work on Addie. He was angry she ever felt the need to punish herself like this. He didn't care if it was a sort of release or done out of anger or self-hatred. It broke his heart knowing that she felt alone and like she couldn't talk to someone about how she was feeling. He vowed to never let her be alone again. He would be here for her.

The buzzing of the tattoo machine sounded through the air. Pop music lightly played in the background. Addie's choice. He let this all be her choice. This was her first step to healing.

Addie watched Ruger closely as he concentrated on his work. She watched as thin black lines were inked into her skin. The pain wasn't close to what she was expecting. In a way, it felt good. She wanted it to hurt; she wanted to feel something again.

"I was four when it started," she said after twenty minutes. Ruger had waited. He wasn't going to push her. He was here to listen. "I don't really remember the guy. But I remember the smell of cheap beer on his breath. He would hit us if we cried. If we begged for help. So I learned to be quiet. Don't move. You'd be okay. You'd live another day".

"I prayed to God every night. Asking him to help me. Asking him to save me". Ruger still didn't meet her eyes. He didn't want her to get scared and stop talking.

"When I was five, I moved out of that home. Ended up somewhere in Northern California. This home wasn't any better. The wife didn't like me. Said I was a brat. That I was too needy. She'd push me away when I tried to hug her. I just wanted a hug." Addie teared up.

"Her husband used to smoke these awful cigarettes. They smelled horrible. My throat would get sore from breathing it every day. He would yell at me and the other kid if we stepped on the grass. We always had to stick to the pathway made of stone. We had to dress properly, not be allowed to look like kids. Kids get messy, Ruger; how do you yell at a child for a little dirt on their pants?"

"My last home was in Fort Worth. I... I don't know if I can talk about that home," she admitted. She absentmindedly picked at the lint on her skirt. She did so like it was more interesting than telling her story.

Ruger could feel her anger and sadness building. If she could admit what had happened to her when she was four, why couldn't she admit what happened at her last home? He was thinking about the worst possibilities. His fingers gripped the tattoo machine a little tighter. His teeth grinding against each other. *'Don't show your anger. Don't scare her away,'* He told himself.

Her head turned towards the ceiling as tears collected in her eyes. "You'll look at me differently," she said quietly, her voice barely above a whisper, "you'll push me away once you know how broken I am."

Ruger sighed and put the machine down on his side table. She needed to know that nothing she would tell him would change his stubborn mind. She needed to know she was safe to tell her story.

"Baby, anything you tell me will never be judged," his voice was stern but sincere.

Addie couldn't look at him. If she was going to do this, she didn't want to see the disgust on his face as she admitted the worst of her history.

"The husband told me I was lucky," she started as Ruger returned to tattooing. He knew he'd need a distraction from her next confession. "I was lucky that someone had taken pity on me."

Ruger didn't quite understand, but he knew she wasn't finished. Addie took a shaky breath as she tried to keep her tears at bay. "I was lucky someone would want anything to do with me because I was a big girl. That I should thank him for raping me. Over and over again," she couldn't hold back her tears anymore. She let them stream down her face as shame enveloped her.

"That I should be thankful I was getting any action since the boys at school weren't interested in me in the slightest." Ruger's heart was beating faster as he tried his best to reign in his anger. His baby. Touched by a man who didn't deserve her. She was a child.

"He would tell me I was ugly, too big to be anything but." Her tears multiplied, "and Ruger, the worst of all, no matter how much I begged him to stop. That I didn't want it. Every. Single. Time. He brought me to release". Sob after sob ripped through her.

"I didn't want it," her broken cries came from her throat as her body shook. She kept her arm as still as she could. She didn't want to mess up Ruger's work.

That was the problem. She cared so much about other people that even as she broke down, she wasn't thinking of herself. She's not worried about messing up something permanent on herself. She's scared Ruger would be upset if he made a mistake.

"That doesn't mean a thing," Ruger huffed. If she could see his eyes, she'd see how dark they'd become. She'd see the murderous rage painted on his face. "It means I'm disgusting and-and broken," she wailed.

"You're far from broken, Addie. What he did to you wasn't right." He'd kill the bastard. He'd do whatever he could to find out who it was and skin him. Hang him by his balls. He didn't care. He'd make him suffer. He'd make sure of it.

"What your body did in that situation? What he took from you. Doesn't mean a thing," he said firmly. He was doing his best to keep himself grounded.

What he wanted to do was whip his machine against the wall. He wanted destruction. He needed it to satisfy his urges. His urges to beat and kill the man harmed the person who meant everything to him. The girl he loved.

"I didn't want it, I promise," Addie hiccuped, "I was a virgin before him." It made sense why Addie was always so nervous to have sex with them. Her only sexual experience besides them was rape.

"I know you didn't want it," Ruger knew it would take more than just those words to prove it. He would spend the rest of his life proving to Addie that she wasn't disgusting or broken; he'd do anything.

"You were just a child. It wasn't your fault," he said softly as his eyes met hers.

"Stop looking at me like I'm broken," she demanded, snapping at the man before her. He was being too kind to her. She expected him to think of her as disgusting, maybe even hate her.

"I'm looking at you like you're my whole world," he replied, "you've never been broken. Not to me".

Addie slumped back in her seat. "You will think that when I tell you the worst of it. I was pregnant. It was his."

"He beat me so badly when he found out. I made it six months before he figured it out. I'd have a four-year-old right now if I had done a better job at hiding it. I could have saved him. My boy."

"Now, I can no longer have children because of what he did to me. He ripped my future away from me. You should be with someone who can give you a child. A real woman."

"That doesn't make you any less of a woman, Addie." Ruger was firm in his opinion that you don't need to be able to have children to be a woman. He wouldn't let her put herself down for something that wasn't her fault.

Her sniffles were drowned out by the music. Why wasn't he just getting rid of her? She didn't understand. She wasn't worth it.

_ele_

For the next few hours, Addie told Ruger about her hope for a future. She wanted to heal. She wanted the fresh start he was giving her by covering the worst of her scars.

"Why do I have to heal from what others did to me?" she sighed. "Because not everyone wants flowers to bloom." was Ruger's response. Poetic.

Addie explained that she hoped she could have a family in the future. Maybe it was too early into their relationship to talk about kids, but Addie couldn't help herself. She had so much love to give to this world. Even after everything bad happened to her, she just wanted to have kids to love and protect.

"After I ran from that home, I ended up in a local shelter with $500 to my name." She had already told Ruger how scared she was to be all alone in the world with nothing but what she had in her backpack.

"I knew I needed to get out of that city. I needed out. So I took my crappy car and drove south. Austin was going to be my fresh start".

"And then that stupid car broke down on the interstate," she rolled her eyes, "luckily Dallas stopped to see if I needed help. Poor thing got scrapped. All I got was $50, but it was enough for food for a few days".

"Then I ended up on top of the bar, and this handsome man picked me up as if I weighed nothing. Like I was a delicate flower. Scratch that. Boston totally manhandled me, and I just let him do it". Ruger chuckled at that, remembering that night well.

"Then this other hot man threatened me when he put me in the back of a truck," she pointed her eyes at Ruger, "but I fell for him anyways."

"And now that hot man is digging needles into your arm," the man smirked.

"Take a look," Ruger asked as he pulled away. Addie stopped talking for a moment to look down at her left arm.

Three yellow daffodils decorated her skin with a singular purple butterfly. Daffodils represented new beginnings, and the purple butterfly would remind her that, in the end, she made it out alive.

"I love it, thank you."

Her new tattoo itched. It was a welcomed distraction from the conversation she was about to have. She knew she needed to do this, but she was scared.

She was scared that her men would look at her differently. She was afraid to lose her happiness again after finally finding it.

The clubhouse was empty beside their group. Cowboy and Boston sat on the couch facing the TV while Addie sat on the edge of the coffee table. She sat between the men's legs. Ruger hung around in the background, leaning against the fireplace. He wanted to give her a chance to do this on her own like she needed to.

Boston and Cowboy were attentive, sitting back to give their girl space to breathe.

"Where do I start?" she mumbled to herself. Why was this so much harder than just talking to Ruger about it? She knew some of his scars and secrets but didn't realize she barely knew the two men before her.

"Start wherever you feel most comfortable. There's no rush," Cowboy said quietly. He didn't want to scare the girl off when she was this close to giving her everything to these men.

"Okay, let's start simple," Boston suggested. They've been together for a few weeks, nearing the end of October. Boston would tell you he knew Addie better than she knew herself, but he also knew that he only saw what she wanted them to see.

"Okay, well, let's start with my age. I'm not actually twenty-four. I know you all saw my ID the first night we met. It's a fake. I'm twenty."

Boston and Cowboy nodded but didn't say a word. Ruger had already relayed that information to them.

"My name is Adelynne Reid, or well, that's what's on my birth certificate. I'm not sure what my name is," she admitted shyly, her eyes pinned to the hole in Cowboy's dark denim jeans. "My first foster family named me, gave me their last name but then didn't end up keeping me for some reason."

She had moved past the hard feelings about being given up by her birth mom and the foster families that came after. "I was never anyone's first choice. I was taken in as mostly a meal ticket. Kids go to bad families, treated like less than a person, and the foster families still come out on top when it comes to the benefits they get because of us."

Boston smiled weakly at those words in understanding.

"I was in and out of different foster homes, through different states. I don't even know where I started out at. They gave me the runaround when I tried to get information on my past homes. Claimed they couldn't tell me anything due to legal issues".

"Several homes were adequate. They fed me, clothed me, and sent me to school. They never hurt me, but I also never felt at home. Never felt safe with them. In other homes, there was violence."

"I was the oldest in one of the homes, and the parents constantly fought. Sometimes it would turn physical, and I would bring the other kids into the bathroom, locking us in there for the night. Too many times, I had them curl up in the bathtub while I stayed with my body trapped between the door and the sink. They would need to get through me to get to those kids. They never once hurt us physically, but there was always the risk,"

Boston looked over at Ruger, noticing how tense the man had gotten. "Some of the homes weren't safe for me physically. For a few years there, I wore more bruises than I did clean clothes. The physical abuse and neglect were hard to deal with as a child, even harder when my social worker didn't believe me. She believed the foster mom, who said I was a clumsy child. The two joked about how it was good that the husband was a doctor." She shivered at that.

"He was never home anyway. He didn't know anything was going on in the home. He didn't know he had married a monster. Or maybe he did. Maybe he did, and that's why he put so many hours into work, to escape her. He was lucky."

Addie breathed deeply before carrying on. Her eyes hardened as she continued to stare at Cowboy's leg. "The last home I was in was the worst. The man was an absolute drunk. Always drinking, never working. There were a few of us in the home. He gave off creepy vibes when I first was brought there."

"I was the oldest of the foster kids there. His eyes would linger on me the longest. His smile was disgusting, yellowed teeth, nauseating breath. I can remember the feeling of his fingernails digging into my wrists as he grew more and more angry. He was almost always angry. I seemed to make him that way."

"I didn't want to do what he asked of me, it made my skin crawl, but it kept the others safe, and in my mind, that's all that mattered to me. They were kids, I was older, it was better this way."

Boston's jaw clenched while Cowboy's mouth twitched. There were so many words they wanted to say to Addie, a mix of wanting her to continue talking about it and wanting to stop her from inflicting more pain on herself.

"I ended up pregnant," she couldn't meet their eyes at the news, "it was his. I started to gather money wherever I could make it or steal it. I needed to get the two of us out safely."

She made a noise like a wounded animal, "I almost made it out. He didn't know I was pregnant until the school called him. I had been in gym class and collapsed. I needed to run, I knew that, but I needed to go back to that house for the money. I had it all planned out."

"He beat me. He ensured I'd lose everything I was trying to save, and then he blamed me for losing the baby. At least after that, he stopped touching me. In a way, I was relieved, but I was also so scared he would move on to someone else."

"He used to say I was his favourite, that I was perfect for him. That I was always so willing, and he knew I would never fight back. But I never wanted it. I wanted it all to stop, but I needed to protect the children."

"And when he stopped going to me, he told me I was broken. He kept telling me he'd give me one last chance, that his son could have me now that I was broken in. That I wasn't going to fight or go to the cops. I never met his son. I could only imagine what kind of monster that man had produced."

She didn't even recognize the tears rolling down her cheeks. "Because of him, I'll never be able to have children. Not only did he take away my baby, but he took away my future." She sucked in a breath before building the courage to meet her men's eyes. "I'm sorry, I won't ever be able to give you guys that kind of future with me. I was selfish not to tell you at the start of this."

Boston's hand cautiously reached out to grasp Addie's chin, his thumb rubbing against her soft cheek. "You're not selfish. You weren't ready to tell us. It took a lot of strength to tell your story." He was acting so calm, touching her so tenderly that a fresh wave of tears hit her eyes.

Her hazel eyes were rimmed red, and tears clumped her lashes. "It doesn't matter if you can't give us children. There are other options, adoption, for example. I mean, hell, if you didn't want kids in the future, we'd be perfectly content with just us."

He wanted to kill the man who caused his girl so much heartache, and with one look at Cowboy, he knew he felt the same way. They'd find the man responsible and ensure he suffered a slow and painful death.

"Thank you for telling us," Cowboy whispered, "telling your story, being so open and vulnerable. That takes a lot of strength."

They looked at her like she was their everything. Their unchanging feelings for her made her feel safe. For the first time in a long time, she was safe. These three men would do anything to protect her. Nothing could hurt her anymore. She was sure of it.

# NINE

The guys had become more protective over Addie. They were more touchy with her. They barely let her out of their sight. Their need to protect her, keep her safe, was immense.

Addie felt safe enough being shadowed by Patriot while working at the bar. She knew the rules. No going into the alley alone or out in the dark alone, no lingering around men not part of the Rising Tide MC. Boston couldn't trust anyone around his girl, but he needed to have faith in the control of his men now that Leon was made an example.

They weren't stupid enough to risk anything. The Prez's old lady? Untouchable. The Vice Prez's old lady? Same story. SGT at arms? Same thing. She was all of theirs. No harm would ever come to her.

Her feet were killing her as the night continued, and she felt low back pain from the heavy lifting she did while helping Patriot unload their delivery truck. She just wanted to curl up in bed with one of her men.

Their sleep schedule was all over the place. She would bounce back and forth between the three men's beds. She hated being away from the two of them, but the one-on-one time was perfect for her and their relationship.

Boston had brought up the idea of getting a larger bed so that Addie would sleep in the same place each night, but the girl wanted to hold off until she felt more secure in their relationship.

Speaking of the man, he had been hovering all day. He looked like he wanted to say something, but every time Addie stopped working and gave him attention, his eyes hardened, teeth clenched, and he'd walk off for a few minutes.

Something was happening with him, and she didn't know what she did to upset him. It had been hard for all of them to hear about her past. Ruger had the time to process the information already. Now Boston and Cowboy needed the same time. It was a lot.

She knew he needed time, yet that didn't stop her from rolling her eyes at the man before throwing her rag down on the bartop and storming off to Boston's office, following the retreating figure. The music muffled the door slam as she closed the two of them off in the man's office.

"Spit it out, Boston; I can't handle this anymore. I'm tired and sore, and you've looked like you needed to talk all day. So spit it out." Her hands found a place on her hips as she stared at the man's back. His head was hung low as he faced his desk.

"I just can't stop thinking about what you went through in those homes. I know foster homes can be scary and traumatic, but I wish someone had protected you like you should have been protected." he sighed.

"I think it's time I told you my story," Boston perched himself on the edge of his desk, motioning for Addie to sit on the small couch to the side. The girl complied, moving to get herself situated.

"My birth mother was a heavy drug user. When I was born, I was taken in by her sister. My aunt managed to raise me for eighteen months before she got sick and couldn't care for me any longer. Cancer took her; from what I was told years later, it was a quick death."

Addie felt bad for the man before her. She knew how drug use could affect the children of users. "I bounced around different homes as you did. During my school years, I moved at least twice a year. Sometimes I was lucky and stayed within the same school or even district. Sometimes, though, I had to start over. I had to learn not to get attached to anyone. It's something I've struggled with."

"I was very fortunate to be in homes where no harm came to me. It didn't mean that foster care wasn't hard on me, because it was. I know it wasn't as bad as it could have been."

The girl nodded in understanding. She always seemed to tell herself that things could be worse, that she was lucky.

"The home before I was adopted was the worst of them all. The foster mom was always laid up in bed. I think she was depressed or something. We hardly saw her. There were two of us in the home. An older girl named Zoe and myself. I think she was freshly seventeen when she came to be with us".

"She was very quiet and tried to keep to herself. I know moving into the house was hard on her. She confessed to me after a few months that she had a baby taken away from her. They separated them. I'm not sure why, but that house was in no way safe for a child, let alone a baby."

"Her social worker had promised she would be reunited with her baby when she turned eighteen and moved out, that this was all temporary."

Addie's stomach clenched at that. She knew how hard it was for her to lose her son. She could understand the anxiety of being separated. She felt horrible for Zoe.

"I was only twelve at the time. I'd hear Zoe cry at night, but I was too young to understand what was going on," Boston's teeth ground as he thought back to that home, "she'd sometimes have bruises on her wrists, fingerprints like someone had dug into her skin to restrain her. Zoe covered them in bracelets or the sleeves of her shirts and sweaters."

"The foster dad had never touched me, never even looked at me the wrong way." his voice deepened as he swallowed, "she tried to tell me what was going on, but I didn't listen. I didn't believe it. I didn't know about all of the evil in the world. I should have tried to help her, but I pushed her away instead."

"Every time she tried to talk to me about it, I'd ignore her, call her a liar. I thought she was saying it to try and get her baby back. Try to be released from the home early. To leave me behind like everyone else had".

"Boston, you couldn't have understood at that age. You were a child too." Addie sympathized. "It's not your fault."

"But her death is." Boston shot back, his words ice cold. The girl before him blinked uncomfortably. She didn't know what to say. "She took her own life because the one person she reached out to didn't try to save her. I should have protected her."

It made sense that with that weight hanging on to the man all these years, he would be overprotective of Addie. It was all clicking together. "You can't blame yourself," Addie said quietly as she reached a hand out to Boston.

"I never wanted to get close to someone else who needed protection. My mom has my dad; he'd die before he let anything happen to her. Cowboy and Ruger can take care of themselves, and Dallas has Ghost. But you, you broke through this wall I had, and I couldn't get you off of my mind."

"I hate knowing you were hurt before. But now, you're safe. As long as our hearts beat, no harm will come to you. Never again will you hurt." He meant it with every fibre of his being. He'd do anything to keep her safe.

Addie stood up, moving between his legs to hug him. Her head lay on his chest, listening to his heart beating. She had never felt safer. "I know, Bos, I know."

# Chapter

## TEN

A ddie wasn't involved in any of the club business. Even though she was their old lady, the guys mostly kept her in the dark. There would be meetings at the clubhouse, always behind closed doors. Dallas would always be put on babysitting duty. That's how Addie had felt about it.

Ghost would always part with a kiss on Dallas' cheek before closing himself behind the meeting room's door. The two girls would hang out. Sometimes baking cookies, watching movies, gossiping, anything to try and distract the two of them from the whispers behind the oak doors.

"Have the guys been acting weird?" Dallas asked her friend as she reached for the bottle of black nail polish from the coffee table. Addie didn't like where she felt this conversation was heading. Yes, they were acting weird, and it had been bothering her. Was it obvious to others that something may be going on?

"That depends; what are you trying to ask?"

Dallas bit her lip, chewing on it out of anxiety. It was a bad habit she had picked up lately. "I don't know, Ghost has been leaving in the middle of the night, and when I try to talk to him about it, he claims it's club business. He won't give me an actual answer. I'm worried he's seeing someone else". Shame enveloped her face.

"Well, I don't think you have to worry about him cheating on you. That man loves you beyond this world. The guys have been crawling out of bed in the middle of the night. I hear whisperings coming from outside the bedroom door. Some nights I can hear bikes coming down the road." Addie had her foot up on the couch as she painted her toes a pale lavender colour.

Dallas' attention flicked back to the closed doors before turning to Addie. "They aren't usually like this. Something big must be going on. This is their way of keeping us safe, I guess."

Addie huffed out in irritation. "How is it keeping us safe when we're kept in the dark?"

"Cowboy and Ghost always said it was better this way. But they've never been this secretive about what's going on."

The younger girl's stomach was becoming tied in knots the longer the men were behind closed doors. She nearly leapt off the couch when it creaked open. Boston was the first one out the door. Determination was written all over his face.

"Get your shoes on, Adelynne," he barked out as he walked past them, heading to the front door. The tone of his voice sent shivers down her spine. She immediately obeyed without question, nearly spilling the glass of water off the coffee table.

Ruger and Cowboy weren't too far behind their president and best friend. Cowboy looked visibly worried, while Ruger looked normal, but Addie could tell the man was pissed off.

Ghost collected Dallas from the living room as Addie and her men shuffled out the door. Cowboy and Ruger both got on their bikes, helmets in hand. "Are they not riding with us?" she asked Boston shyly.

He was in a mood, and it worried her. Ever since she had told them about her past, he's been different. Distant even. "We're taking our bikes. Have you ever been on one?" he questioned as he grabbed a spare helmet for Addie.

"Yes, well, it's kind of the same idea as a bicycle, right?". Boston stared at her blankly with his hands held out with the helmet. He was dumbfounded by her response. She had only ridden once on the back of Dallas' bike.

"I mean, I guess?"

Addie snatched the helmet from his hands, throwing it over her head. Her cheeks were rosy from embarrassment, and she wanted to hide away from his stare.

Boston let out a quiet chuckle before swinging his leg over the bike. He put his own helmet on before twisting around to face Addie. "Be careful, don't need you getting hurt, love."

Her chest pressed into Boston's back as she slipped onto the back of the bike. She was worried they would lose balance and crash onto the ground. She'd hate to scratch one of their bikes. She knew just how protective they were of those bikes and their cuts.

"Wrap your arms around my waist and hold on tight." Boston's right hand tapped Addie's hands as they clasped around his middle. Her face rested against the back of his shoulder. She liked this. Felt like she was just giving him a big hug.

The wind whipped at them as they rode along the highways. It was a beautiful Autumn day, and the leaves started changing colours.

The closer they got to Cowboy's family farm, the more anxiety grew in her body. Boston had looked annoyed when they walked out of their meeting. What was going on?

The call of their motorcycles coming up the driveway was enough to gain the attention of Cowboy's parents. Pam and Richard were out in the garden, harvesting carrots and potatoes.

Pam's face was covered in dirt from where she had rubbed it with the back of her gloved hand. Confusion was the first emotion Addie could make out before a bright smile worked its way to her face.

She dusted her hands off on her overalls before peeling her gloves off. Boston climbed off of his bike before helping Addie to her feet. She realized that Ghost and Dallas had followed behind them.

Dallas was as confused as Addie was. "Why are we here?" the older girl asked her brother as she parked her bike beside his. "Sure, I'm glad to see Ma and Pa, but something is going on, and I don't like it. I don't like being left in the dark".

Cowboy frowned at his younger sister before looking over at Addie. It was better this way. To keep the girls in the dark. "Ghost says he hasn't been bringing you out here to practise shooting, that you need a refresher. And I'm sure the only time Addie's picked up a gun was when she nearly shot Ruger."

Ruger smirked at the memory as he pulled Addie into his side, "my little spitfire," he cooed in her ear before kissing her temple. The idea of his woman pointing his own gun at him was very hot. He loved it, knowing she couldn't pull the trigger.

"Oh good, you're all here!" Pam squealed in excitement as she approached the multiple bikes, "Not that I don't mind random visits, but what's the occasion?"

"We need the space for target practice," Cowboy explained, kissing his mother's dirt-covered cheek. Her eyes pointed at Boston. She knew a bit about what her boy was involved in, and as much as she loved Boston like he was her own, she still didn't like her son being involved in it.

"Lyle, I do hope you're keeping my kids out of trouble," she tutted the tall man. "As always, Ma. Never will I let something happen to any of them," he replied.

Cowboy had a favourite spot for shooting practice on the farm. It was far enough from the house and barn that it wouldn't bother his parents or the animals. But it was cleared enough that they could practice at straight shots.

It was Texas, and everyone was packing heat. Still, Addie never really paid much attention to the holster on the men's sides before. She looked apprehensive as she faced her men.

"We just want you to be safe," Boston explained, "we need to make sure you can keep yourself safe if we aren't around. We've kept you in a bubble long enough, but we won't always be there to save you."

"Don't look at it like you're scared," Ruger chided as he held the gun out to her, "not like you haven't pulled this exact one on me before."

"That was one time," she pouted as she stomped her foot, "I was somewhere I didn't recognize, and you cavemen were stomping down the hall while yelling at Dallas."

"Don't start acting like a brat," Ruger warned the girl, "this is for your own safety."

Boston, Cowboy and Ruger stood around Addie while Ghost and Dallas were already practicing. Dallas had years of experience but didn't go shooting often. So she had a head start on Addie.

"Besides that one time, have you ever actually held a gun before?" Cowboy asked. His voice was sweet. He wasn't being condescending.

"Only water guns, but never an actual weapon," the girl replied. A blush rose to her cheeks as Ruger chuckled, "So you mean to tell me, even if that gun had been loaded, you couldn't have shot me?".

"Well, don't you just pull the trigger?" It seemed simple enough. Aim the gun, pull the trigger.

"The safety was still on," Ruger smirked, "so I guess the first lesson will be how to release the safety."

"See the little switch above your thumb? Flip that." He instructed. When she did as he asked, she heard a light click. "Now what?"

"Now, you'll aim at what you're going to shoot." He encouraged her as she aimed towards the hay bale with a paper target.

"Then pull the trigger." With a bang, the corner of the paper was blown off, and hay flew in the air. She was a lousy shot.

Addie swung around excitedly, and her men ducked to the ground. "Finger off the trigger!" Boston yelled to Addie as Cowboy and him hit the ground.

Ruger's eyes darkened as he disarmed his girl. Grabbing the gun by the barrel and pointing it to the ground as he pushed her hand away. He immediately put the safety on.

"Maybe the first step would have been to tell you not to swing a loaded gun around," he said as he holstered his weapon.

"I wasn't going to shoot you," she protested. "Maybe not on purpose," the man replied.

Addie stomped her foot again as she turned to face Boston and Cowboy, "So you three dragged me out here after acting all secretive, let me get one shot in, and that's it? That's not fair. Why does Dallas get to shoot off more than one round? How am I supposed to protect myself if I don't know what I'm protecting myself from?"

She was acting bratty, and she knew it, but she couldn't stop the words from coming out of her mouth.

Boston went to speak, but Ruger cut him off. "Why are you acting like such a brat?" he asked in a low voice.

"I'm not acting like a brat. You're just being unfair. This isn't fair!" She finished her sentence by banging her fist off Ruger's chest.

A light growl was heard coming from the man. His hand gripped her wrist, trapping her against his chest. "You don't need to act like a brat for me to fuck you like one," his words barely above a whisper.

Addie whimpered at his words, giving up her fight. She didn't even know why she was in such a mood. She knew the guys would tell her what was going on. They had never given her a reason to not trust them.

"Seems our girl is a little wound up," Ruger explained to his friends, "I'll get her settled, and we'll be back to continue." They nodded their heads in response as they removed their guns from their holsters.

"First one to hit the target wins. The other owes them a beer," Cowboy chuckled. His warm gaze landed on Addie, "You know he'll fix your attitude, right?".

Addie looked away from Cowboy. Not saying a word, she was beyond embarrassed. She wouldn't stop Ruger from taking her away for a few minutes. She wanted this more than she had realized. Was that why she was so cranky?

Ruger led Addie over to the barn to the right of them. As soon as they were out of sight, he pressed her body against the weathered wood. "I like you better in skirts," he huffed, kissing down her neck. His hand trailed between their bodies, settling at the top of her black leggings.

"Why?" she asked as she closed her eyes. Falling victim to this feeling, to his lips. "Because it's easier when I need to fuck the attitude out of you."

He tugged at the waistband of the leggings, pulling them and her panties down at the same time, letting them settle around her knees. His fingers met her wet heat, pride filling his chest. "I knew my girl needed me. Catching an attitude all because she's a desperate little whore, what a shame."

"What a shame?" she asked, confused as the tip of his finger circled her clit. A shiver of ecstasy travelled through her. "It's a shame you couldn't just use your big girl words and ask for my cock.".

A second finger added pressure to the sensitive bud, flicking back and forth. Her mouth opened like she wanted to moan, but she held it back. Her friends and her other two boyfriends were around the corner of the barn. She didn't want to be loud.

"We could get caught like this," Addie began as Ruger pulled his hand away. He used the slick on his hand to rub at his shaft. He didn't have time to prep her. She'd have to be thankful he was taking care of her right now anyway.

"Cowboy would never let his family see you like this," Ruger assured, "and I'm too possessive to risk anyone seeing you come apart like this. Anyone but us."

"You're going to be a good girl and beg, and you better hope I'm the forgiving type."

Her eyes widened as she stared up at Ruger's near-black ones. The domination in his words nearly made her cum.

She was going to beg. She'd get down on her knees and pray to God if it meant she'd get the satisfaction of Ruger fucking the attitude out of her. This man had ruined her. She was feral for the words he spoke.

"Ruger, I need..." she begged as she tried to press her body closer to his. Ruger slammed her back against the barn boards.

"What you need to be is fucking thankful I'm taking mercy," he growled before kicking her left leg out, widening her stance to allow himself room.

The tip of his cock ran between her folds. Her sweet nectar coated him. Before Addie could continue her pitiful begging, Ruger thrust forward. His rigid member stretched her wide as she took him deeper.

Her head found a place in her man's neck. Her fingers dug into the material of his shirt. The breath was knocked out of her as he relentlessly pounded into her body.

"Ruger," she whimpered as she tried to get a handle on herself.

Sex with each of them was different. Cowboy was sweet and dominating but could make her cry from his lovemaking. Boston was in control but worshipped her body. Sex with Ruger was different. It was primal even.

"You like being fucked like this. Your pussy is clenching around me so fucking hard. Trying to milk me of my seed," his hot breath fanning the side of her face, "that's what you want, isn't it? What you crave?"

"Need you, crave you," Addie mindlessly repeated. So overrun with pleasure she could barely think. Her moans were muffled by the skin of Ruger's throat. But it was still enough to spur the man on.

Every little breath, whimper and moan, Ruger controlled. This was all his doing. "I'm going to cum in you, and then you'll be a good girl again and practice shooting. For your own safety." He ground out as his hips pistoned.

He shifted his hips, and it was enough to cause a cry to fall from Addie's lips. She was so close. Ruger could hear the sound of slick skin gliding together. Could feel how tightly she was squeezing him.

His lips trailed kisses along her jaw, moving down her neck. Dark red splotches were left behind. He was going to mark her for everyone to see. He should fucking tattoo his name on her. Make her his in every way so everyone knew she was forever off the market.

Ruger's hips stuttered as he came, feeling Addie reach her peak right behind him. Her head slammed back against the barn as she cried out. Her eyes rolled into the back of her head.

He knew, at this moment, that he could never let her go. She was his forever.

# Chapter ELEVEN

Storms raged on outside the clubhouse, while an even darker one raged war inside of Addie. The skies were lit up from each strike of lightning. The zig-zagged bolts illuminated the fields surrounding them.

Thunder rolled in waves, the aftershocks rippling through Addie's chest. At this point, she couldn't tell you if the shaking was from the vibrations of the thunder coming through or from the constant anxiety building steadily through her body.

With each crack of thunder, the girl jumped, her body pulling flush against Boston's. Her protector tonight.

Boston's arms wrapped around Addie's waist as they cuddled on the couch. It was the third night in a row that she couldn't stay in bed all night. Something was wrong, and she couldn't tell what.

Anxiety plagued her, and nightmares had come in abundance the last few days. Her tummy twisted and turned. She knew she was becoming a nervous wreck the less she slept.

The first night, Cowboy had tried to soothe her back to sleep with a calming bubble bath. He knew warm showers helped him when he was having a horrible night, and he knew Dallas loved bubble baths, so he hoped Addie was the same.

Lavender and vanilla invaded her senses. The bubbles covered her pale skin. With her head leaned back against the edge of the tub, Addie tried to block out the world. She sat in the bath until the water turned cold—her teeth chattering and skin pruny. The anxiety was still there. It was a nice gesture, but it didn't help.

The next night, Ruger and Addie split a bottle of wine and watched a movie marathon to take her mind off of things, hoping it would help. The sparkling wine was an odd thing to witness the rugged ex-marine partake in, but he'd do anything to make his girl happy. She ended up a giggly mess but was still anxious.

No matter what her men had tried, it felt as if nothing could help the girl. It was frustrating for Addie. She didn't want to feel like this.

Boston was considering bringing her to a doctor. His mom was a therapist and knew that sometimes people just needed extra help from medication to live an everyday life. He just wanted to help his girl, and with a past like theirs, he knew she might need to talk to somebody.

He knew it took him a while to adjust to living a normal life once he was out of foster care. It hadn't hit him for a few months after he moved in with his adoptive parents all that he had been through. Addie had only been out since late July; barely even three months had passed.

Boston's story wasn't nearly as tragic as his lover's. He escaped with barely a scratch. He believed he was very fortunate to come out with a family that loved him. His parents and extended family never treated him differently. He was theirs, even without the blood.

Boston took a look at the time on his phone. The light from his phone screen illuminated his tired face. Addie could have sworn the man looked like he was aging rapidly due to the lack of sleep and added stress.

It was nearing two in the morning. He knew his mother was probably asleep already, knowing it was around midnight for her. "Baby, I'm going to make a call quick," Boston warned Addie, "I think I know someone who can help."

Addie frowned but nodded her head. She played with the fingers of Boston's left hand as it rested on her stomach. With his right hand, he dialled the one person he knew would be able to help.

"Lyle? Are you okay, sweetie?" an older woman's voice called out once the ringing had stopped. "I'm okay, Mom," he assured her. His mother was always concerned about her son. He remembered when he scraped his knee when falling off his bicycle. She hauled him inside, nearly in tears, as she picked out the grass and rocks from his wound.

"Not that I don't want to speak with my favourite son, but what do I owe the pleasure of speaking with you at.... almost midnight?"

"Well, I guess something is happening, and I was wondering if you could help us?"

"What do you need?" her voice was so sweet it broke Addie's heart. She had always wanted a mother, begged and cried and prayed, but she wasn't fortunate enough to have one.

"My girlfriend is dealing with a lot of anxiety and can't sleep. It's been a few days, and I don't know how to help." He felt like he was failing Addie by not knowing what to do.

His mom was quiet for a moment. "There's probably not much that can be done tonight besides being there for her. But I'm more than happy to speak with her and fit her into my schedule for weekly appointments if she'd like. Talking to someone can be greatly beneficial for mental health."

"Is that what you'd like to do, Baby? Would you like to talk to someone? Maybe it will help."

Addie had never been able to see a therapist, and now she had no insurance to pay for it. "I don't have insurance. I'll be okay," she already felt guilty she had been keeping her men up, not even in a fun, sexy way.

"She wouldn't take your insurance if you did. She's offering to help," Boston explained, "as a favour to me."

"Oh," Addie was shocked. He'd ask his mom to help her because she was his. "Only if she doesn't mind," she added as she bit on her plush bottom lip.

"Can we set something up tomorrow?" Boston asked his mom with a warm smile on his face. "Of course, I'll video call when I'm free."

"I called my mom last night," Boston told his friends in the morning. The smell of freshly brewed coffee wafted through the air. His mug on the second refill of the brown liquid. "She's going to talk to Addie today. Not the way I wanted to introduce them, but I know it's for the best."

"Do you think we did something to stir this all up," Cowboy asked worriedly. He hated feeling helpless when someone he cared about was suffering. "She was fine before we took her to the farm to learn how to shoot," he added.

The red-haired man shook his head. Sadness was evident in his eyes, like a tsunami. "I dealt with anxiety and depression when I moved in with my parents before they adopted me. It was the first place I truly felt safe. I think that Addie's going through the same thing. She's safe with us."

The girl stumbled into the room blindly as she rubbed her tired eyes. She had managed to get an hour or two at most of sleep.

Boston had been on this indie coffee kick, and in Addie's mind and nose, the coffee smelt like cat piss. Her nervous stomach rolled as soon as she inhaled the scent. "Enjoying your cat piss?" she hissed out as she dry heaved.

Boston cut her an irritated look. They've been arguing over this coffee for a few days now, the man already ready for another go around.

"This coffee cost me $35 a bag. I'm using it until it's gone, so get used to it, Buttercup," Boston responded as he took another sip at his cup.

The less Addie slept, the more irritable she had become. She was angry as her darkened eyes reached Boston's stare. If he wasn't so in love with her, he would have snapped back harder.

Tears were forming in her eyes as she stomped her bare foot on the floor. Ruger's eyebrow cocked up as he watched the scene unfold between his best friend and lover.

"I'll pay you to fuck off," she growled out. Cowboy's eyes flickered across the room. Their girl had never sworn before. Now all of a sudden, she's just dropping the f-bomb.

"Oh really?" Boston countered, "You really want me to go away?".

"Yes! You're so infuriating to even be around. Always picking fights, always being mean. I don't understand it; if you hate me so much, why don't you just leave?".

Boston's tone had been level and calm the whole time he had been speaking to Addie. None of the men brought up how she was constantly picking fights with their leader. None spoke a word about how Boston had always been kind to their girl.

"And you two," she spun around and pointed at Cowboy and Ruger, "you never stand up for me when he's being mean. What, just because he's your big, bad leader, means you're going to just allow him to speak to me like that?"

Before she allowed any of her men to say another word, she rushed out of the kitchen, ran up to her own bedroom and slammed the door shut. She was just tired. So tired.

Addie still avoided her men. She needed to sleep, but her brain just wouldn't shut off. Every little noise from downstairs caused her to jump.

It didn't help that the club was still having secret meetings and keeping the girls in the dark. It also didn't help that sitting on Addie's own dresser was a Glock meant for her to protect herself with.

She was beginning to feel like a mouse, hiding away in her room all of the time. When she left the clubhouse, she stuck close to her lovers. She never left their sides.

She was both clingy and distant, adding to the confusion between them all.

# Chapter TWELVE

S he had done a couple of sessions with Mallory. She greatly liked the older lady, but Addie felt she was wasting her time. When she wasn't at work, she curled up in bed. Her own bed. Not Cowboy, Boston, or Ruger's. Hers. In Dallas' old room.

Mallory said this was normal. She was withdrawing from the people she found safety in. Mallory claimed it was part of the healing process. Boston understood that better than anyone else, but it was still hard on him.

"How long do we have to sit back and watch this go on?" Ruger asked as his eyes flicked over to the staircase. He was annoyed, not at Addie. This wasn't her fault. He was upset because there wasn't anything he could do to fix this situation.

"We wait until she's ready," Boston explained as he sipped his whiskey. The golden liquid swirled around the cup in his hand. "We'll know when she's ready. She'll return to us," he nodded, assuring his best friend.

"Bye, Mallory. Thank you again for today. I'll see you Thursday," she said politely to the older woman on the screen. Boston's mom was a sweetheart, but she was also very good at her job, and Addie was thankful she had made room in her schedule for the girl.

When Addie emerged from her bedroom, feet hitting the wooden floor, she felt different. She felt determined. She felt good. Real good. Happy even.

The stairs creaked with each step as she made her way toward the chatter from her men. She knew they were talking about her. The men had been nervous about what this meant for the four of them.

"Cowboy, we've got to go to work, or we're going to be late," she singsonged as she moved past the couches and to the front door where her shoes and bag were, "I don't think the Boss will be happy if we're caught slacking!"

Work hadn't really changed with Addie's moods. She still gave 110% to her work. Counting inventory may seem boring for anyone else, but she felt useful. Like she wasn't wasting everyone's time. It was something others would brush off, but it was a job she was proud of.

"So, we've officially picked a day for the wedding," Dallas blurted out as soon as Addie walked back into the main part of the shop. Inventory and ordering were now pushed to the back of her brain as her eyes widened at her friend. "When is it?" she asked happily.

Cowboy watched as the girl glowed, if even for a moment. It was a glimmer of the girl he had fallen for. He was going to savour the moment.

"November 14th, it will be exactly 6 years to the day he first asked me out." Dallas' smile widened. Her eyes sparkled with tears, "he picked the date. Doesn't November 14th sound perfect?".

"Dal, that's like two weeks away!" her friend gasped, "We're going to need to find you a dress and rings!".

"I don't care if I have a dress or rings. All that matters is I have my family and friends close by." Dallas assured. That's all that mattered in the end.

"Will you be there with me?" she asked her friend as she turned to walk back towards the hog she was working on. Dallas was a mostly sheltered child, raised on the family farm with just her brother as her only friend. When her brother met Boston, her friend group had grown slightly.

Her friends were really friends of her brother, but they treated the MC Princess well. Besides Ghost and the rest of the club, Dallas had no one. She now had Addie, the one person who wanted to be her friend for her and not because she was part of the club.

"Will you be my maid of honour?" She continued. Dallas brushed the curls falling in her face as she peeked at Addie. The other girl was shocked. "You want that to be me?" she asked cautiously. Scared if she was too loud, then Dallas would change her mind.

"I need it to be you. Because you're my best friend." the smile on her face was bright, warming the air. "I couldn't do this without you," she added.

"Of course, I'll be there for you!" Addie was already coming up with different ideas for a bachelorette party. She was going to make it memorable for her friend.

"Good. I'll admit, I was a little scared to ask you," she admitted as she grabbed a wrench and turned her focus to the motorcycle she was working on. "I was worried it would be too much."

In a way, Addie understood what her friend meant. They hadn't known each other long and still couldn't believe they were friends, no strings attached.

Dallas had been used by a few ex-friends who only gave her the time of day so they could get closer to club members. Addie had never been close to anyone. Never feeling worthy of friendship. She had stuck to herself mostly in school. This was her first friend, and she didn't want to lose her by being too much.

Addie's eyes welled up with tears as she recalled the last few months. All of the good changes in her life. Things were starting to look up. She still dealt with a lot of anxiety, some days better than others, but Mallory had explained that those feelings were normal.

Her brain had been in survival mode for so long that she didn't know how to live without it. Dallas and the club were slowly chipping away at those feelings. She was starting to feel safe. It was normal for her to instinctually try to destroy the first taste of safety she's ever honestly had.

"I love you, Dal. I'm so happy for you and Ghost." She truly meant it. Dallas was the second person she had ever loved. Her first was the child she had lost. Dallas was the closest to an actual family member she had. The older girl treated her as more than just a friend. She was her sister too.

"I love you too, Ads. Forever and always," she nodded as her lips curled. She tried to hold back her own tears. They both truly meant it. "I will always be here for you, no matter what. I've always got your back."

Cowboy's heart was beating a mile a minute watching the interaction. He tried to peel his eyes away from the two girls to give them some privacy, but he couldn't. His baby sister finally found a friend who was here for the long run, and he was so thankful that Addie was bringing the softer side out of the girl.

He knew she had trust issues and that Boston and them had only worsened them. They did what they thought was best to protect Dallas from their world. They let her dip her toes in the water but never allowed her to thoroughly drench herself in the club business.

She didn't trust others well. On two hands, the girl could count those she trusted. Ma, Pa, Boston, Cowboy, Ruger, Ghost, and now Addie were among them.

Cowboy's eyes met Addie's, and he saw the happiness shining back through them. He knew his girl was still in there, and he was ready to do anything to keep her happy and safe.

Addie's eyes flicked back to look down at Dallas as she sat on the stool. "So I need to know, what colours? Cake? I need details." she giggled.

Dallas and Addie discussed wedding plans for the next four hours while the two Caville siblings worked on their bikes. Cowboy's earbuds had been put away long ago, and he just happily listened to the two girls talk about anything and everything.

"Come on, you two," Cowboy called out as he stood up, wiping his hands on a towel. "It's getting late, and Addie promised to help out at Tide Rising tonight for a little bit."

Addie knew it would be a long night, but she knew Patriot would appreciate the help tonight on Halloween.

"Come on, Dal, I know you gotta get home to Ghost and get ready. We're going to have a blast tonight," Addie could already imagine the trouble the two girls would get into. Cowboy only rolled his eyes.

## THIRTEEN

C owboy had dropped Addie off at Tide Rising before heading out; he needed a shower and change. Her outfit was already in Boston's office, waiting for her to get ready.

She made her way through the growing crowd, noticing some of the club's old ladies were also there. She squeezed past the occupied pool tables and slipped into the hall. The women's bathroom door opened, and a witch and a vampire walked out. They definitely just fucked in the bathroom.

Once she made it into Boston's office, she spotted her outfit. White tennis shoes and white knee-high socks were in one bag. In the garment bag laid across Boston's desk was a white tennis skirt and a baby pink cropped polo shirt.

This outfit was solely Boston's pick. His parents were wealthy Californians who spent most of their free time at the membership-only Country Club. Boston was thrown into the life of a rich boy with daddy's money.

They were rich Catholics who were surprisingly down-to-earth and friendly.

She pulled on her outfit, knowing the skirt barely covered her ass. She knew all three of her men would be here tonight, so she was okay. She was safe.

Her tips definitely skyrocketed tonight, and she wasn't sure if it was purely from her outfit or because it was a holiday, but Addie wasn't complaining.

Patriot was dressed up as a sexy cop. He was definitely a hot sight for the ladies. Addie had caught her partner flirting away with a few lucky girls.

Addie knew the moment her men walked into the room. The three men's faces were covered, but Addie knew them well enough to know they were hers. They had come here for her.

Boston, Ruger and Cowboy wore similar outfits, sporting a different colour mask. The LED masks hid everything but their eyes.

Boston's was green, Cowboy's was blue, and Ruger's was red.

Their outfits were black tactical-looking outfits, most likely Ruger's choice. She knew what was in store for later that night. The boys had been teasing it for a few days. She could not wait until they left here, but first things first, their business needed to be taken care of.

Addie didn't even know what happened. One moment, she was bent over, sweeping up broken glass, and the next, there was a fight behind her. Two drunk guys were punching at each other. A girl was yelling and screaming at them to stop.

This was definitely not the first fight she had witnessed at the bar, but it was the one that was closest to her. She was trapped between the end of the bar and the corner with no way out.

Her eyes wide as she considered jumping over the bar to the other side. "Ruger!" she shouted over the music, looking for the scariest of her men. She knew not to intervene ever. That was Boston's rule.

Within 30 seconds, the bigger man of the two was pulled back, an arm hooked around his throat. Ghost had grabbed the smaller guy and held him back by the arm.

"Did you really think it was a good idea to start your pissing match in our bar and scare my girl?" Ruger asked dangerously as his arm dug further into the guy's throat. "My girl is supposed to be safe here. Did we not learn from dear old Leon?"

"I'm so-sorry," the man stumbled out as he looked Addie's way. "Eyes off her buddy," Ruger spat as he hauled the man to the door.

Ghost followed suit with the other man. "I don't want to see either of you here again. And kiss your spot in the club goodbye."

When Ruger walked back over to where he was chatting with Cowboy, he could see the lust written all over Addie's face. He knew she liked what she had witnessed, but it still pissed him off that she had felt even slightly scared.

———ele———

She was so needy it hurt. These three men had indeed ruined her. Before them, she wasn't too interested in sex; now, now she couldn't get enough.

It was a busy night, everyone bustling about. She should have been tired after her shift but was happy to be here.

She stood beside Boston, a slight blush on her face. She could do this. No one would hear her ask. "Baby, what's going on in that pretty head of yours?" he asked sweetly, unaware of her problem.

"Sir," she bit her lip. She knew she was soaked from watching Ruger stop that fight. The way her men demanded respect was such a turn-on for her. The name had Boston checking her over.

Seeing the flush on her cheeks, he knew what was going on. With a smirk, he met her gaze again. Her hazel eyes clouded with need. "Does my baby need me to help her out?" he cooed.

Addie nodded as she looked down at the truck keys on the table. "Nu-uh baby, I have another idea. Get Ruger and Cowboy, and then come here," he ordered. His smirk grew darker as she huffed and walked away. Oh, he was going to make this good for her.

Boston knew it was dark enough in the corner booth that no one would see what they were doing, but he wouldn't risk Addie's safety like this.

Ruger and Cowboy nodded at Boston as they followed behind Addie, neither knowing what was happening. "Boys, our sweet little girl is feeling a tad touch deprived, isn't that right, sweetie?". Addie nodded, her blush deepening.

"She needs me to take care of her. Mind blocking us from view?" Boston winked. He knew the two other men would do anything for Addie. Boston didn't even need to ask.

Addie gasped. "He-here?" her eyes widening. "No need to act all modest, Baby; we know you like the risk of someone catching you. Such a naughty girl".

"You're going to climb on Bos' lap, sweets, and ride his cock good," Cowboy whispered in her ear before biting down on it lightly. A moan spilled past her lip as Ruger kissed up her neck, "Let him cum inside you so you have a reminder that only one of us can satisfy you."

The three men had a strange fascination with knowing their cum had filled their girl. It was animalistic, but it always made

Addie's orgasms even better, so who was she to deny them the right?

"Keep your skirt on, but take your panties off," Cowboy ordered. From where Ruger and Cowboy stood and under the darkness, no one but her three men could see her pull her black lace panties off. She allowed Ruger to take them and stuff them in his back pocket for safekeeping.

Boston had already unbuttoned and unzipped his pants, running a thick hand over his cock. "Come here, Baby, let me make you feel good".

Addie crawled onto the booth with Boston. She allowed the man to help situate her. She looked back at Cowboy and Ruger, watching their eyes darken before they turned around. Their backs to their lover, their eyes scanning the bar. Nothing looked out of sorts this way.

"Take me in slowly," Boston breathed out as he peppered kisses along Addie's jaw. The girl took him inch by inch, going slowly. After months together and with three of them, she still couldn't take them without giving her time to adjust.

She bit her lip to muffle her moans as Boston stretched her out. The feeling was delicious, and her eyes rolled back as she was fully seated on his lap.

"Do not silence those noises. I want to hear everything". Boston's hand pulled Addie's head into the side of his throat. "Only we can hear. Move when you're ready. The boys got us covered".

Without another look at her other men, Addie raised herself just enough. She was taking her time, savouring this moment.

With her back against his chest, her hands dug into the table before her to keep herself steady. Her knees stuck against the leather bench, her skirt covering them the best it could.

"Bos," she whined out as she ground down onto the man. She tried to quiet herself by kissing his neck. His face was still covered by the black mask. She could only focus on the green string light on his mask.

"Such a good girl, Baby, so good," Boston praised as his hands roamed her body. His hands rubbed against her thighs. His right hand trailed between her legs to rub at her clit.

Addie's legs quivered as she gave in to the feeling. As Boston realized she was struggling to keep up, he shoved her forward. Her chest pressed against the top of the table as he took over.

"My dirty girl, begging to be fucked. To be filled, where anyone could see her." Boston groaned, "You're taking my cock like you were made to. Come on, Baby, cum with me," he said through gritted teeth as Addie squeezed him harder.

Her cheek pressed against the table as she came. Boston fucked her through her climax, his thrusts speeding up before reaching his own.

—*ele*—

Addie giggled as she stumbled, getting out of Boston's truck. Cowboy's arm reached out to settle the girl. It was nearing three in the morning, and Addie had a few too many Halloween-themed drinks.

The girl barely registered that they were on the other side of the woods surrounding the clubhouse. The truck was shut off as the men slammed their doors shut. With their masks sitting on top of their heads, Addie couldn't really see them in the dark.

A nervous laugh spewed from her lips as she whipped around to look at them. "Aren't we going inside?" she questioned.

"We've got a surprise first, Adelynne," Boston started, "You should really learn to stop reading those dirty books where everyone can see. You're not very discreet about it."

She had no idea what the oldest man was talking about.

The three men slipped their masks back down. "If I were you, I'd be running," Ruger chuckled darkly, "it's what you wanted, right?"

That's when it clicked. Ruger had taken her phone the other day at work when she had gotten turned on, and he read what she had been reading. Three men in masks stalking their victim. It shouldn't have been hot, but Addie took off running.

It reminded her of their time at the farm when they had first told her to run. She needed to go on daily runs or something, or she was just too drunk, but this was definitely harder in the dark.

The only lights she could see were the men's masks as they spread out. At least she had an advantage. She could see them, but they couldn't see her.

"This will be fun," Addie said quietly as she watched her step. Excitement and anxiety ran through her. A bubble of laughter erupted from her throat.

Shhh. She needed to be quiet.

"Oh, Adelynne!" Boston called out as the three stalked their way through the woods.

Addie's head whipped to the call, seeing her men gaining on her. She was confident they couldn't tell exactly where she was, but they were close.

Her tennis skirt flared as she ran, her shoes pounding on the ground.

"Gotcha!" Boston growled as he pushed Addie against a nearby tree.

"Such a good girl wearing what I left out for you to wear," he continued, "walking around looking like a perfect little slut".

"I want a good look at her panties, Bos," Cowboy said as he stepped on a stick. The sound cracking in the air.

Boston's right hand stayed splayed in her back, keeping her pressed against the tree, his lift hand flipping her skirt up.

"She really does have a fine ass," Ruger grunted as he neared.

Her black lace panties were soaked with her arousal. Addie wiggled, trying to see if Boston would lessen his hold, but he didn't.

— *ell* —

She didn't know how she ended up in Boston's bed. All she knew was that her head was pounding, and her stomach was rolling.

The taste of alcohol mixed with bile on her tongue as she launched out of bed. The sheets tangled around her feet, nearly tripping her.

Her head hung low by the ceramic bowl as she heaved.

Last night's drinks and her dinner came up, and before long, she was left dry heaving. Her hair was pulled back from her face as she felt someone kneel beside her.

A large hand rubbed at her back while she cried. Addie wiped at the spit on her lips with the back of her right hand. Did she really drink that much that she was throwing up everything?

She had promised herself she wouldn't get that drunk again, but obviously, that didn't work out.

"I'm never drinking again," she groaned, leaning back against her man's chest. Boston.

The man didn't have his glasses on, and his long hair was messy. Addie would have tugged him down to meet her lips if she hadn't just been throwing her guts up.

"I've heard that before," the man chuckled as he pressed a kiss to Addie's temple. "Let's get you back into bed. You need more rest."

## FOURTEEN

The drive to the farm had become a comforting one. Cowboy's parents had welcomed Addie in with open arms. His mother always ensured Addie was fed and happy. At the same time, his dad told her heartwarming stories about Cowboy and Dallas as little kids.

Jealous wouldn't be the word Addie wanted to use, but his whole life seemed perfect. The family farm was in excellent condition, with plenty of room. They were like a family plastered across magazines. Everything about them was perfect.

Dallas and Cowboy were lucky in many aspects. They had each other but also loving parents who would do anything for them. The Caville's lived the American dream.

It may be small-town living, but it did them well.

Addie watched out the window, exclaiming "cows" whenever they passed a field with them in it. Cowboy's eyes would flicker towards Addie. A smile grew wider on his face. He enjoyed seeing her so happy and carefree.

They had taken the day off at the shop. Cowboy knew how freeing being at the farm was, and he wanted to take her there. Get her out of the clubhouse, out of the bar, somewhere she could breathe without everyone waiting around for the other shoe to drop.

Mallory had told the guys that fresh air and sunshine could heal anything. No matter how much trauma someone endured, it could heal a person, even if just temporarily. It was an escape and a much-needed one at that.

They had left the more dense neighbourhoods of the small town outside of Austin, driving deeper into the countryside towards the Caville family farm.

Every twist and turn in the road was ingrained in Cowboy. This was where he grew up. He knew them like the back of his hands. He could swear he could drive blindfolded.

With the windows down and the late fall air flowing through the truck, Cowboy took a deep breath. The country air filled his lungs. Besides the smell of farm life wafting through occasionally, it was as fresh as possible.

Addie's right hand hung out the window, the cooler air zipping over her skin. Goosebumps formed up her arm.

She was still mostly lost in her head, but Mallory was proud of how well she'd been doing. She'd been coming back out of her shell. It took multiple appointments with her for Addie to start gaining some positive coping skills.

*"No more running,"* Boston had ordered. He did all he could to keep her head above water while she learned how to save herself.

The driveway was a long one with dust kicking up behind the tires. Addie and Cowboy were tossed around as they drove over the rocks. It was a comfort to Cowboy. As he had grown older, the farm had become more of a safe space for him. Something he had craved.

Instead of parking along the side of the house like usual, Cowboy kept driving around to the barn. The building could use a new paint job, but it was sturdy and beautiful to Addie.

"What are we doing back here?" she asked as she turned to look at Cowboy. He had picked out her outfit. A pair of well-fitting jeans and a chunky knit sweater. On her feet were the cowboy boots the VP had bought for her months before her first visit to the farm.

"I'm going to teach you how to ride," a toothy grin spread across his face, "I haven't been riding in forever. I'm sure Diesel has been itching to go riding."

Diesel was a beautiful, all-black horse. Addie didn't know much about horses but knew this one was gorgeous.

"He's been mine since I was a boy. Born to one of the horses we had before. We lost her when she gave birth to him. So Ma and I took turns caring for him. Bottle-fed him and everything."

Cowboy made his way around the barn, grabbing his riding gear. It, too, was all black.

"We'll get Diesel all ready to go, and then we'll get your horse all set up."

"My horse?" Addie asked, confused. There was no way she was riding a horse on her own. Couldn't she just ride on the back of Cowboy's?

Cowboy's head nodded to the stall beside Diesel's, "Take a look. Ma picked her out for you. She's supposed to be a smooth ride and is used to beginners," he explained.

Addie's heart stopped when she peaked in the stall. If she thought Diesel was gorgeous, she had no idea what to think about this horse. Her coat was rust-coloured, and on her forehead was a white patch shaped like a heart.

"She doesn't have a name yet. I figured you'd want to name her." Cowboy walked up behind Addie with another set of riding gear. This set was brown with yellow sunflowers embroidered on it.

"Oh, well, you should name her," Addie said as she backed away a little. "Why? She's your horse?" Cowboy's eyebrows knit together in confusion. Did she not like the horse?

"I bought her for you," he added.

"Wait, you bought me a horse?"

"Figured it would help, and I thought you'd like to be my riding buddy? I read up a bit on equine therapy." He shrugged like it was no big deal. But to Addie, it was. It meant a lot that all her men were trying to help in their own ways.

Addie's heart swelled as he spoke. He had really thought through this. He really wanted to help her.

"Well, I guess you better teach me how to ride, Cowboy," she teased before her hand cupped his face, pulling him down to place a kiss on his lips.

"Nice and easy now," Cowboy said with a smile as they neared the embankment's edge, "this was always my favourite place to stop when I rode more often."

From here, they could see the neighbouring town they lived in. The leaves on the surrounding trees were starting to turn colour, rustling in the breeze. It was picturesque, a little slice of heaven.

"It's beautiful," Addie admitted as she took in her surroundings. They had been riding slowly, allowing Addie to learn how to ride and to take a breather from life. Real life.

"I would come here to think," Cowboy explained, "even when I was a little boy and things at home were tough, I'd take Diesel here, and we'd ride around, eventually ending up here each time."

"I know you must think that my life was perfect compared to Ruger and Boston's. I can't possibly understand anything you've gone through, but I lived through enough to sympathize."

Addie's eyes moved from their view to her man. He adjusted his black cowboy hat as he spoke. "Ma and Pa had a rough going when I was young. Pa drank a lot. He never hit us, but he was a drunk."

"My parents are high school sweethearts. They've known each other since they were in diapers. They were always destined to end up together. It was fate."

Cowboy reached down to pat Diesel's head, running his fingers through the dark mane.

"Pa was a football star. Even got a full ride to college to play. Ma was pregnant with me at the time. She made sure she attended every game. As cheer captain, that was her thing, but she would have shown up anyways for Pa."

"Right before graduation, Pa was injured. His knee was never the same again, and he wasn't able to play. Their future to get out of this small town was stripped away from them. Their one chance to get out."

"So, he did what plenty of others do when their dreams of a future seemed squashed. He drank. That's all he ever did. He could barely keep a job. Ma worked at the local diner to keep food on the table and a roof above our heads for most of our childhood."

"Why didn't she take you and Dal and just leave?" Addie questioned, her heart breaking for the kids and Pam.

"She loved him too much. She would tell me that the Richard she fell in love with was still in there somewhere. That he needed to battle his demons, that he would come back to us. So she stayed. She stayed by his side through everything."

Addie stayed quiet as she listened on. Her heart beat fast as Cowboy continued.

"He turned into a good man. He treats her right and treats us well. He got sober." Cowboy added, "I vowed to be more like my Ma than him. I vowed to always stay through everything.".

"I thought I was becoming a coward. I met a woman around the same time I had met Boston. She seemed to hang around the bar often. I now know she just wanted to dig her claws into a biker."

"She was everything I thought I had wanted in a woman. In the end, she played me. I was torn up really bad when she left. I thought she would be my old lady, my whole world."

"She was pregnant, which led me to believe it was mine, but it was some prospect's. She played me for a fool. Made me look bad to the whole club, but I didn't even care about that. The future I thought I had with her was torn away. The baby I had spent months preparing for wasn't my blood, but I was determined to do right by him and step up."

"For months, I begged and pleaded for her back. I swallowed my pride. I would have been a father to that little boy. The guys had to snap me out of it."

"I became irate when my head started to clear, when my heart was starting to heal. I took it out on everyone around me. Ma, Pa, fuck, even Dallas felt my wrath. I was a monster for a little while... but I've had time to battle my demons."

"Why are you telling me all of this?" Addie questioned, her eyes trained out on the field in front of them.

"Because you need to know that we all understand your demons. We understand that you need time to battle them. We're not going to let you go."

"Give your everything to me. Every broken, tainted, and cruel part of yourself. Give me your sunshine and rainbows. I want your all. I want your everything."

"Being free means not allowing anything to wear you down, not allowing anything to take up space in your mind and heart that aren't worth it. That's freedom."

After a moment or two, Addie turned back to Cowboy, "I feel free."

## FIFTEEN

"**G**ood Afternoon, Ronnie!" Addie called as she walked into the sub shop. The smell of freshly baked bread wafted through the air and nearly had Addie drooling.

"Addie, what do I owe the pleasure of seeing my favourite customer on this fine day?" the older gentleman called out as he pulled new rolls out of the oven. Sweat formed on his forehead from the heat of the appliance.

"Just picking up dinner for the shop. How have you been? It's been a few weeks." Addie had been improving with her mental health and decided to walk down the block to see Ronnie on her own.

"I've been good. I was getting a little worried that your biker friend was keeping you away from here. Does he know you've come here?" the older man's eyes flickered to behind Addie's head towards the door.

Addie frowned at that, "No, why?". Ronnie wiped his hands on a clean tea towel.

"He doesn't like you coming around. Made a huge show of it and scared off some of my customers."

Why would Ruger do that? "I'm sorry, Ronnie." Addie said quietly, "I don't know what's gotten into him lately."

"Are you safe with him?" Ronnie huffed out, "he's controlling, yes, but is he hurting you?"

Addie flinched at the older man's tone. "Ruger would never hurt me," she protested, "he just wants me to be safe and happy."

"Well, you haven't looked happy in a long while."

Addie didn't want to get into this with Ronnie, so she decided that changing the subject was a better tactic. "Zach will be coming to visit soon, right? That'll be good for you."

Bringing up the man's grandson was a good idea. The man loved the boy and loved talking about him at any moment. "Yeah, I can't wait to see him. He said he'd be helping me out around here for a few days. You should stop by again and meet him. He'd be good for you, unlike that shady biker you associate with."

"Ruger's not shady," Addie said with a roll of her eyes, "you just don't know him well enough."

They fell silent as Ronnie made the usual sandwiches, only speaking to give Addie the total before she left.

"Take care of yourself, Addie, because no one else will."

"Bye, Ronnie."

Ruger only grunted when she placed his sandwich on the counter behind his workstation. He was focusing on a back piece for one of the bikers. Viper, she thought his name was.

She had already dropped off the food for Molly, Wes and Marco. She thought something was off. Wrong. Ronnie was being weird.

"Can we talk, Ruger?" Addie asked quietly. She bit down on her bottom lip in worry. Something wasn't right.

Ruger looked up at Addie, the tattoo machine still buzzing in his hand. He could see that something was bothering her. He knew what he needed to do.

"Viper, we're going to have to finish this up another day," Ruger said as he pushed back on his stool, "my old lady needs me."

"That's alright," Viper replied as he lifted himself up, "I'll see you again in a few weeks to finish this."

"Sorry," Addie mumbled as the man gathered his things before leaving. Ruger nodded towards his office as he removed his black vinyl gloves.

"No need to be sorry. I was about ready to tap out myself. Can only take so much in one sitting," the man winked at Addie.

Ruger said his goodbyes to the man before patting him on the shoulder, "Don't let that shit get infected, Vipe, I think it's some of my best work."

"Don't need to worry. It's not my first rodeo!" The man called out as he walked away.

Addie and Ruger made their way to the man's office. The man let her walk in first before shutting the door behind them.

"What's going on, Baby?" Ruger asked softly.

Addie was torn between being upset that Ruger had confronted Ronnie and being concerned that Ronnie was being a little off.

"Did you stop at Ronnie's lately?" she started. Being direct was best with Ruger.

"Depends, what did that old man say?" his jaw clenched as he spoke. He really didn't like the man.

"That you scared away some customers and told him you don't like me being around there."

Ruger rolled his eyes as his arms crossed against his chest. He leaned against the edge of the desk. "He needs to mind his own business. Tell me, what else did he say? I'm sure he had a lot to say about me to you. How I'm controlling and manipulative? That I'm unsafe to be around?"

Addie swallowed hard as she heard the tone Ruger spoke with. He was getting angry. She wasn't scared he would hurt her, but she hated knowing she was upsetting him.

"He was acting weird. Talking about how I needed to protect myself because no one else will." she sighed. Twisting at her fingers to calm herself, Addie focused on anything but Ruger. "He seems to think I'm being hurt or going to get hurt... I don't know. But I feel like something bad is going to happen".

Ruger pulled her close as he kissed the top of her head. "You're safe; nothing will happen to you, not on my watch. I'd die before any harm came to you. You know that."

"I just want to get home. I just have a bad feeling that I can't seem to shake," Addie admitted, "Take me home, Ruger?".

"Anything for you. Get your things."

Boston looked displeased as he watched Addie sleep. She was curled up in Ruger's bed, the blankets nearly covering her face. He adjusted the glasses on his face before turning to look at Cowboy and Ruger.

"I never liked the fucker," Boston started, "but now he's getting our girl all worked up and we can't have that."

"I tried playing nice for Addie's sake. I warned him to stay away from her." Ruger was annoyed that the older man didn't listen.

"Ruger, keep a closer eye on her at the shop. I have no idea what he's up to. But whatever it is, I'm sure we won't like it".

Addie's arms wrapped around Ruger tighter, squeezing her body as close to the man as possible. She was nervous, and her nightmares plagued her. The eyes that haunted her memories kept merging with Ronnie's face. She could smell the scent of stale cigarettes and the booze on the monster's tongue, but she was seeing Ronnie's face.

"It's okay, it's okay," she heard a man coo as he tried to calm Addie down. Her thoughts were racing like her heart rate. She tried to hurry further away from Ruger in her half-asleep state, nearly toppling to the floor.

Ruger kept his arms wrapped around her to keep her on the bed. His lips peppered kisses along her cheek and neck, hoping she'd wake up enough to calm down or wear herself back out.

It felt like all of their progress was going down the drain. It was like they were starting at stage one again. But he wasn't giving up. He would never give up on her.

"I'm here; you're safe."

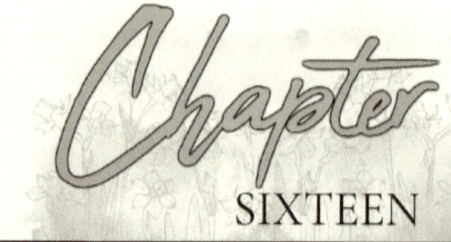

# SIXTEEN

E veryone was bustling around, trying to get last-minute items taken care of. Cowboy was running to the floral shop to pick up the flowers. Boston was taking apart the shelves in the fridge to store the cake for the ceremony. Ruger was helping Ghost get ready, while Addie helped Dallas.

Pam was in tears as Addie focused all her attention on Dallas' makeup. "I can't believe my little girl is getting married," Pam wept.

Addie had to ask three times if they were happy tears before she had been comfortable continuing Dallas' eyeshadow. Browns, greys and blacks were swept across her eyelids. Dallas' makeup was typically dark around her eyes, and that's what she wanted for her wedding day. With the smokey-looking makeup, her eyes popped.

"Ma, it's not like you're losing me. I'm getting married, not dying," Dallas chuckled as she tried not to flinch while Addie applied a coat of mascara on her lashes.

"I know, I know," Pam patted at her eyes with a crumpled tissue, "but it just means that my youngest is all grown up now. I don't know if I'll get this with Reuben. This may be the only wedding I get from you both."

Pam had meant well, but it still hurt to hear her say that. Addie and Cowboy had only been together a few months; she shouldn't even be considering getting married anytime soon. Throw in the complication of the other two guys, and Addie realized that Pam was right. This was the one wedding she'd get from her kids. Unless Cowboy moved on.

Tears stung at her eyes as she turned around to busy herself with digging through the makeup bag.

"Ma!" Dallas hissed as she came to Addie's defence.

Pam realized her mistake in wording and immediately felt her heart breaking. "Oh, Honey, I didn't mean it like that," she rushed out, "it's just..." she trailed off. She didn't know how to take her words back.

"It's complicated," Addie supplied, "I get that." She couldn't hold the slipped words against Pam. This was a different kind of situation than most people typically encountered. It was tough.

Dallas' eyes cut to Addie's. She could see the pain and sadness in her hazel eyes. "Do you think you could help me into my dress?" Dallas asked Addie, trying to change the subject.

That snapped Addie out of her little pity party. She needed to focus. This was her best friend's wedding day, not time for her sadness.

Immediately, her mask fell into place. A warm smile coming out. "Of course," she replied sweetly. "I'll do the finishing touches when we get you into your dress. Everything should be ready soon!"

Dallas smiled back as she stood up from the edge of her old bed, now Addie's, fixing her satin dressing gown.

It's not that Dallas felt like she was walking on eggshells. She just hated seeing how sad Addie would get on occasion.

The night before, Addie and Dallas had been drinking. It was a mini bachelorette party, just the two of them. Addie admitted that it was coming up to the anniversary of losing her baby and that she was just sad about it.

Addie unzipped the garment bag holding her best friend's wedding dress. They went for something subtle, but Dallas through and through. The southern sweetheart would not be caught dead in a white dress, so her dress was a black lacey one that hugged her figure perfectly. It was initially meant to be a prom dress, but with the right accessories, it worked perfectly for Dallas' wedding.

The younger girl helped her friend get dressed before doing up the zipper, moving her dark curls out of the way. The fabric clung to all the right places, and Addie thought Dallas looked like a dream.

Addie was dressed in a dark red satin dress. It wasn't something she would have chosen herself, and if it wasn't for it being Dallas' special day, this dress would have never left the closet. It was tight on her, hugging her curves. She felt uncomfortable that her body was displayed like this, but Dallas loved the fit and told Addie that she needed her maid of honour to look like a snack.

Whatever that meant.

*ele*

Ghost and Dallas had decided on a small, intimate wedding. Something between the close members of the club and their families.

Ghost's small family consisted of his parents and an older brother.

As Addie walked through the kitchen, she could see outside the sliding doors. She could see the chairs that were set up and the makeshift aisle. You wouldn't think that a bunch of bikers could come up with this beautiful and simple event, but they had managed.

Black and red roses lined the aisle, extra petals sprinkled on the grass. The red oak and maple trees by the front were different shades of red. Boston, Ghost, Cowboy and Ruger stood at the front, all in their cuts, each with a rose pinned to them. Ghost's was black while the others were red.

Boston would be performing the ceremony for Ghost and Dallas, and it was a sweet offer from the club's president.

"You almost ready to go out there?" Addie turned to look back at Dallas, "Ghost will die on the spot once he sees how smoking hot his wife looks."

"I'm just hoping we make it through the ceremony before my brother or his friends haul your fine ass away," Dallas replied with a wink.

Richard walked into the kitchen a moment later while Pam fussed about with Dallas' hair one last time. "You ready, Sweetheart?" Richard asked as tears welled up in his eyes. He was giving his baby girl away.

"I'm ready, Pa. He's the one," she assured the man.

"Then let's get this over with before I change my mind," he joked before linking his arm with hers.

Pam walked out first, throwing rose petals down on the grass. Addie was next, with a bouquet of flowers in her hands. She was glad they all had decided on flats because she would have tripped walking down the aisle on the grass.

Richard and Dallas were the last ones to walk down the aisle, following behind Addie.

Addie couldn't help but notice the three pairs of eyes landing on her. It was evident that her men liked what they saw, and maybe Dallas was right. She looked good enough to eat.

Ghost's eyes were focused only on Dallas and how beautiful she looked. His whole world. His old lady. His everything.

Richard placed a kiss on Dallas' cheek before going to sit beside his wife.

It's not like Addie had meant to not pay attention to the whole ceremony, but she couldn't take her eyes off of her men. She could barely hear a word that Boston had said and only snapped out of it when he told Ghost he could kiss Dallas.

She had been daydreaming about what it would be like to get married, but she knew that was impossible with the three men. How would something like that work?

Cowboy's arms snaked around her waist, pulling her in close. "You look so fucking sexy," he growled out. He was quiet enough that no one else heard but loud enough that Addie swore she was already dripping wet.

Ruger crowded around Addie from behind, his head tucked against her throat as he breathed in her scent. Addie whined as he began peppering kisses along her skin.

She was mildly aware that there were others around, but she was trapped between two of her men. Her eyes opened and met with Boston's as he stood talking to Viper, one of the members of the club Addie had come to know.

His eyes darkened as he watched his two best friends working the girl up. He could see the blush on her face and the need in her gaze.

Addie watched as Boston said his goodbyes to Viper before working his way over to his small group.

"You better find yourself in one of our beds, and when I find you, I'm going to fuck you like I mean it," Ruger gritted out.

Giggles spilled from her lips as she tore from her men. Rushing towards the house, Addie met Dallas's eyes, and the other girl winked. She knew what was about to go down as she witnessed her brother and his friends calmly but surely following Addie.

Addie kicked off her flats in the kitchen before running up the stairs. The fabric of her red satin dress bunched up in her hands as she ran.

She could hear the guys running up the stairs behind her. She ran down the hall, not stopping until she threw open Boston's bedroom door.

The door was slammed shut in a split second, and she was pushed against it. The bottom of her dress slid up as her leg was hitched up.

Cowboy's rough hands held her still. His hardening cock against her lace panties.

"I swear I'm going to burn all of your baggy clothes and only let you wear shit like this," he said harshly as he nipped at her lips. "You look so fucking sinful."

Cowboy never really spoke like this. He was always the sweet, Southern gentleman. But the way Addie looked today made him throw that away, wanting to devour her.

"Who knew Cowboy could talk like that?" Boston chuckled, "Must have gotten him all wound up, Baby. Going to let him show you how perfect you look?".

Addie's hazel eyes reached Cowboy's piercing blues. Her chest rose and fell as she breathed deeply.

As her mouth opened to say something, anything, a shout came up the stairs. "Reuben! Lyle! Judas! Addie! Get your asses down here. We're cutting the cake!" they heard Dallas yell before laughing.

She knew she was being a cock block, and Addie couldn't help but roll her eyes. "Looks like we're needed elsewhere, boys." She laughed herself as she slid out from Cowboy's hold.

# SEVENTEEN

"Come on, that's not fair," Addie pouted up at Cowboy. It was a reasonable question, and the stubborn man's answer was no.

"I just want to learn. I promise I won't crash or something."

She wanted to learn how to ride a motorcycle. She wanted to feel like she fit in their world. "Dallas knows how to ride, why can't I?"

Cowboy pinched the bridge of his nose. Boston would kill him if Ruger didn't make it there first. He was pained. Stuck between a rock and a hard place.

"Dallas does what she wants. Plus, she built her own bike," he huffed out. Addie looked so sad, and he couldn't stand it. He wasn't worried about the motorcycle; he was concerned about her safety. Her bottom lip quivered, and that was enough to break him.

"Fine," he threw his hands up in the air as he gave in, "I'll teach you to ride, but don't be pissed off at me when I'm slaughtered for teaching you."

He loved his friends; they were like brothers to him, but he didn't love their wrath. At all.

He really shouldn't be doing this. He was asking to be murdered. Asking to be skinned alive or something horrible.

Addie's broad smile and the sparkle in her eyes was worth it to him. He'd take a beating, he'd die, whatever he had to do to keep her safe and happy.

She was so excited she could barely keep herself contained. She clapped her hands together happily as she rushed over to Cowboy's bike. The black beauty glistened in the sun.

"Now, you get a scratch on her; you have to fix it," he warned as he gathered her helmet.

As soon as he walked over to Addie, he helped the girl secure the helmet over her head. He was silently happy that she was begging to learn on a day when she was wearing jeans with a matching denim jacket. She'd be protected if she wiped out. Plus, the alley-way had a low-speed limit. Even if she hit the ground, she'd be fine.

He also considered making her wear knee and elbow pads but felt it may be overkill. He was sure he could probably find some if he dug around in his office if he really wanted to.

"First, you need to learn the parts of the bike before you get on," he started as they stood around the motorcycle. Dallas watched on from where she was seated, taking a water break. A smirk plastered on her face. Her brother was whipped.

"These are the handlebars," Cowboy continued, "they help you steer." He pointed towards the front of the bike.

"No, shit," Addie grumbled. She felt like Cowboy wasn't going to take this seriously.

His eyes cut to Addie, a warning laying behind the striking blue colour. After a moment of silence, challenging Addie to say another word, Cowboy returned his eyes to the bike.

"As I was saying, the handlebars. The throttle is in the right one. You speed up by twisting it towards you slow down by twisting it away. When you let go, it goes back to its original position."

"This here is the front brake lever. It will brake the front wheel if you squeeze it. The rear brake lever is down here by the right footrest." He pointed towards the footrest.

Moving around the bike to the other side, Cowboy pointed at the left handlebar. "This is the clutch. You pull the clutch to change gears, squeeze to disengage."

"Down here is the shift lever. You use your foot to move the lever up or down to choose which gear you want to be in."

"The ignition switch and starter actually start the bike. The starter button is on the right handlebar by the throttle."

"Always, always, do a safety check before riding," he said sternly, "especially for someone who isn't an experienced rider, you don't know the bike well enough to save yourself if something is wrong."

"Tires, fluids, headlight, taillight, turn signals, battery," he ran through a list, using his fingers to count, "brake light, clutch, throttle, mirrors, brakes and..." he trailed off before he hit the horn, "horn, for when assholes try to cut you off." Addie rolled her eyes at the man. Silently thankful he was actually taking things seriously.

"Now, this isn't like driving a car. You're the smallest thing on the road and with the least amount of protection. You can easily end up in someone's blind spot. You can very easily get hurt."

Why was Cowboy such a mother hen?

"Because this bike has a kickstand, get on from the left side and use your foot to kick it up. Then, you can center yourself. Both of your feet should be able to touch the ground like that." He instructed, giving Addie a moment to follow through.

"Good, now turn on the ignition switch. Yup, just like that," he nodded as Addie followed his instructions, "shift the transmission to neutral. Mhm."

"Squeeze the clutch and press the start button. Good, good." The motorcycle roared to life.

"Now show me the brakes and throttle. I need to know that you remember this. They are important. And I won't let you ride until you remember them."

He then proceeded to explain how to switch gears. He knew Addie was itching to ride, but he was glad she hadn't said a word. She needed to understand how important this was for her safety and that of others.

She was determined to learn and not make a total fool out of herself. When Cowboy gave her the go-ahead, she took a few moments to build the courage to actually move the motorcycle.

The bodyshop was down an alleyway, so it was safe for her to practice. There were rarely any cars on the road here.

Cowboy wasn't nearly as worried about his bike being damaged as he was worried about Addie losing control. She wasn't going very fast, but he didn't want as much as a scrape to mare her skin.

"She's going to make you go old quick," Dallas laughed as she approached her older brother. His arms were crossed over his chest as he watched Addie zip up and down the alleyway and through the parking lot.

Cowboy looked over at his sister, "Every grey hair I get from her is worth it."

He was so in love, and everyone around them could tell.

"She's good for you, Rue. She's good for all of you. Lyle and Judas needed her, too." Dallas loved Addie like a sister, but no matter how much she loved the girl, Cowboy's heart had hers beat.

"It's only been a few months, Allie, but she's the one I see a future with," he admitted, "I'm scared to ever lose her. She's the missing piece I didn't know I was looking for. She's my world, all my stars, my universe. Everything I do from here on out is for her."

"Her safety. Her happiness. Her everything."

"You're good for her, too," Dallas added. "She doesn't like talking about what happened to her in life. She's too proud to talk about it. It's like she pretends nothing happened, so it can no longer hurt her anymore. She acts like nothing can touch her because she wants to move forward."

"Mallory has been a big help. I can't take all the credit."

"You've given her a taste of freedom," Dallas pointed out, "she knows how good it tastes now. That's why she wanted you to teach her how to ride. I heard you brought her to the farm. I know you told her the truth. About how you're finally free from your own demons."

Cowboy kicked at a rock by his foot before adjusting his hat. "I never wanted to get close to another woman, Al. It was just supposed to be me and the boys. No old lady, nothing. Not after her." He still couldn't bring himself to speak her name, "that shit doesn't just leave easily."

"Who would have thought that the Rising Tide MC badasses would all get an old lady as sweet as Addie?" Dallas hummed, "She really is good for you all. She keeps you on your toes and humble."

"No, you keep us on our toes," Cowboy chuckled as he bumped his shoulder into his sister.

"Always." She promised, holding her pinky up to promise her brother, just like when they were young.

His pinky linked with hers. A silent promise between the siblings.

"What do you mean you taught her how to ride?" Were the first words out of Boston's mouth as soon as Addie dropped the bomb. Cowboy stood behind Addie in the living room, his back leaning against the fireplace.

Addie's eyes were wide. She didn't honestly believe Boston or Ruger would be mad at Cowboy for teaching her. She was obviously wrong based on the looks of anger painted on both of their faces.

Ruger remained silent as Boston looked ready to murder his best friend. Addie's mouth parted as she tried to fix the situation she started. Trying to put out the fire before her.

"He wasn't going to, but then I pretended I was going to start crying because he said no," she added quickly, hoping that admission would calm things down. All it did was add more fuel to the fire.

"She did the lip quiver thing, and you just gave in?" Boston laughed darkly, "You didn't even discuss this with us? Just making life or death decisions on your own?".

Cowboy scoffed and pushed off of the fireplace. "It wasn't life or death. It was just a joyride around the parking lot and down the alleyway."

"You're being dramatic, Bos, I'm not a child." Addie pouted as she stabbed her pointer finger against the tallest man's chest, "You can't treat me like one."

"I can do what I want," he huffed as he looked down at her, "Your safety is my responsibility."

"It's mine too, Boston. If it were up to just you, she would be bubble-wrapped and kept away from knives and high places. Give it up; let her live a little," Cowboy replied with a roll of his eyes.

"Shut up," Ruger ordered, "I hate hearing you two bitch about everything. You're worse than two girls going at it".

"So what, she learned to ride, big deal? Am I happy about it? No, but is it really a big deal that you two are going at each other's throats about it? No."

Addie's excitement for learning a new thing was squashed by her men, and they didn't even notice the girl stomping away and slamming her bedroom door. Tears rolled down her cheeks. She was so proud of herself, but they were more worried about treating her like a child.

She would show them.

# EIGHTEEN

B oston had been pestering Addie all day. "Baby, just give me his name," he pleaded. He wanted justice for everything Addie had been through. He had let it go for too long and needed to know who harmed her. He needed to fix her. To help her heal.

"It doesn't matter, Bos, he can't hurt me anymore," she replied.

"But what if he's hurting others? What if you weren't the only one?" That was a low blow.

Addie winced at the words, pulling herself from his arms and sitting on the edge of the bed. They decided to try to nap before Cowboy and Ruger returned from helping Richard at the farm.

Addie had wanted to go but had been irritable all day with a raging migraine. Her sleep schedule hadn't been the greatest lately, and nausea bubbled in her stomach due to the pounding in her head.

She just wanted darkness and silence. Boston wasn't giving up, though.

She didn't understand why he couldn't give this up. There was nothing that could be done to fix what had happened. She just wanted to move on.

He hated that he was upsetting her, but he needed to do something to help her.

"Bos, my head hurts, and I don't feel good. Can we just drop it? I don't want to fight with you".

Boston sighed as he sat up against the headboard. "Fine, I'll drop it for now. Do you need anything for the migraine?".

"Pain reliever would be great. In a box under the sink in the bathroom," she explained as she pulled her arm over her eyes.

She heard Boston rustling around under her bathroom sink before he returned to the bedroom. In one hand, it was her migraine medication; in the other was an unopened box of tampons.

"Didn't we buy these after you moved in?" he asked slowly. Addie looked over at the box, confusion forming across her features. "Yes?" she questioned.

For a moment, the two were silent. Addie could barely think over the pounding in her head.

She had always had a regular cycle. With everything that was going on in her life, she hardly thought about the box of tampons. The ones she hadn't opened yet.

"It's been what? About two and a half months since you moved in? Almost three?" Boston continued.

Addie realized what Boston was implying. She sat up quickly on the bed, tugging the sheets around her tighter. "No way. There's no way," she spluttered.

She couldn't be pregnant. The doctor said it was impossible. She had told Boston, Cowboy and Ruger that it wasn't possible. That would make her out to be a liar. Like she had trapped them. Or at least one of them.

"Doctors aren't always right..." As he approached the bed, Boston said calmly, "I can run and get a test, then you'll know. Maybe that's why you haven't been feeling good".

"All you need to do is pee on it and then wait a few minutes," Boston explained as Addie sat on the toilet. She glared up at the man, "I've done this before, Boston." She didn't mean to sound rude, but the girl was scared.

Boston kneeled in front of her, grabbing her hands with his. "No matter what the test says, this doesn't change a thing," he assured her.

"Cowboy, Ruger and myself will still be here. Even if positive, we'll stand by you," it was a promise.

"What if I am? Then that means they'll think I lied to them. That I'm trying to trap one of you".

"You could never trap one of us like this. We could have taken precautions, yes, but this isn't the end of the world. We'll work through it."

Addie hiccuped as she took the test from Boston's hand. She made quick work of what she needed to do before placing the test on the counter.

"You have my word, no matter what happens. If you're pregnant with our child, they will never end up like us. No matter what. They will never end up in the system. They'll have four parents instead of two and a huge family who will love them. If something happens, they'll never be on their own".

The timer Boston had set went off on his phone. "I can't look," Addie admitted, "it will change everything if I am.""

"Do you want me to look first?" Boston offered. When Addie only nodded in response, Boston grabbed the test off the counter.

She knew what the test said the moment Boston's arms wrapped around her. He placed a kiss on her forehead, muttering the words, "Nothing will change."

Tears steadily streamed down her face. She felt like a failure, like a liar. Her whole body trembled as she sobbed. What was she supposed to do now? Pack her things and leave? Make it easier for the guys to get rid of her?

She had some money, but it felt like it wouldn't be enough. She couldn't run again. She couldn't give her baby up for adoption. She was worried she would be repeating the cycle.

"I'm never letting you go, either of you," he promised quietly as he rubbed at her back, "Cowboy and Ruger would say the same."

Her eyes were rimmed red and puffy from all her tears. The pink test was heavy in her right hand. Heavy with her future.

"This might not have been something any of us had planned, but maybe it's something we all needed in our lives," Boston's voice floated into the living room where Addie was now seated.

He had carried her down to the couch, helping her cover up with a big blanket.

She was scared, but Boston told her that they couldn't have secrets like this and that she needed to be open and honest with the other two guys.

She could hear the sound of two bikes pulling up along the house. They were home. And Addie felt like she was going to throw up. She wasn't sure if just from nerves or the baby.

Cowboy and Ruger walked through the door a moment later, their laughter filling the air. Ruger noticed Addie sitting on the couch, upset at first. His laughter dying out.

"Baby, what's wrong?" He asked as he walked over to his girl, "What happened?" his eyes flickered to Boston's as the man walked around to sit on another couch.

Cowboy walked calmly towards Addie, not wanting to spook her. She looked ready to run at a moment's notice.

"I'm pregnant," she mumbled quietly. Boston wanted her to do this on her terms, so he wasn't taking over telling his friends the news.

"I didn't quite hear you, Honey," Cowboy said as he squatted before her.

"I said, I'm pregnant," tears stung at her already sore eyes. Cowboy and Ruger took a moment to digest what she had just said.

Their eyes locked on Boston's as he nodded his head.

This changed nothing. She was theirs, and they wouldn't let her run off now.

"Not sure why you're crying then, Baby," Ruger said with a widening smile, "I think this calls for a celebration."

# NINETEEN

Addie tossed and turned all night. She couldn't sleep, and it was tormenting her. The little bit of sleep she had gotten was stolen away from her by a bad dream—a nightmare.

Really, it was a memory. A horrific memory. One her body still vividly remembered. Every touch, every grasp, every terror beating through her chest. Her mind so badly wanted to forget, but her body would always remember.

She had awoken with a gasp, her hands flying to her stomach to protect her unborn child. Tears sprung to her eyes as her head whipped around, looking out into the darkness.

She tried to stay quiet while looking for the devil in the dark. The one who would crawl into her bed as a girl. The one whose breath stunk of cigarettes and beer. The one who had haunted her every few weeks since she escaped.

Would he find her one day? Would he harm her unborn child? Would she ever really be safe?

Boston's arms wrapped around the girl as he tried pulling her closer to him. His hand blindly rubbed at her back. "It's okay," he assured, "you're here with me."

A sob plummeted from her lips as she cried. She was safe. She was with Boston.

She took a deep breath, breathing in the man's calming scent. She was safe.

Bile rose up her throat, and she tried to swallow it back down. "I'll never be safe. Our baby will never be safe. He will find me," she cried.

Boston sat up, blindly fumbling for his glasses as he did so. Nearly knocking them onto the floor. "Who will find you?" It was the middle of the night, and he rubbed the sleep from his eyes.

The December storm raged outside. The rain hit the windows while the lightning illuminated the sky.

Addie's knees were pulled up to her chest, her arms wrapped around them. Shame fell over her like a blanket.

"My foster father. He warned me that I could never escape him, that he would always find me." Her eyes shined bright with tears, "I'm scared he's going to find me."

Boston held the girl close as he tried to calm her down. "I need you to give me his name. So I can know who I need to protect you from".

"His name is Tommy," she finally admitted.

The silence in the room was enough for her to hear only the beating of her heart.

Boston went ridged at the name. His heart dropped into his stomach.

"Tommy Kline," she explained as she rubbed at her eyes, willing the tears to stop. This was the first time she had ever spoken his name. It tasted bitter on her tongue.

Boston moved his arms away from Addie before getting up off of the bed. He walked over to his closet, pulling on a pair of black sweatpants and a shirt.

"Where are you going?" Addie asked worriedly as she watched the man hurry around the bedroom.

"I need to take care of something. I'll be right back," he assured.

Addie followed the man down the stairs. "Sit on the couch," Boston ordered lightly, "Ruger and Cowboy will be here with you. Club business. I'll be back," he continued as he placed a kiss on Addie's lips.

The man left, heading into the storm. Addie could hear his bike roaring to life.

Cowboy and Ruger made their way down the stairs, both in just sweatpants. "You okay, baby?" Ruger asked as he approached his girl on the couch.

"He's been asking for a name for weeks, and as soon as I opened up, he left. He said he had to deal with club business," She looked torn apart.

Ruger and Cowboy quickly masked their looks of confusion. They focused on keeping Addie company.

They discovered that Addie was about 15 weeks along in her pregnancy. She was showing only slightly at this point. The only ones who knew were the parents, Ghost and Dallas.

They were waiting until Christmas day to announce to their families and the club. Addie looked over at the Christmas tree they had put up. Colourful bulbs and lights adorned it: her first tree and her first Christmas in safety.

Ghost and Dallas trudged through the front door. Sleep was lost amongst them all. It was going to be a long night, Addie felt.

Ghost, Ruger and Cowboy excused themselves to the meeting room, closing the oak doors behind them.

"How are you feeling, Honeybee?" Dallas asked as she curled up next to Addie on the couch. "Scared," she admitted as she rubbed at her small bump.

"Boston's going to make it right. He's going to fix this. You'll never need to be scared again," Dallas promised.

That's when it clicked in. Boston wasn't going out in a storm for some club business. He was going out to protect Addie.

She jumped off of the couch, pushing Dallas away in the process. She scrambled for her boots before pulling them on her feet.

He was out for revenge.

Addie grabbed her gun from its box by the front door before running out. She needed to stop him from doing this.

She grabbed Cowboy's bike, ignoring Dallas' pleas not to do anything stupid.

She remembered Cowboy's training and started the bike. Peeling down the driveway, the rain pelted down on her. Her pj top and bottoms were sticking to her skin.

She could vaguely hear a second bike start-up after her, following her. Dallas.

She had no time to look back at her friend. She needed to get to Boston. He was making a mistake. He was going to get hurt.

As Addie raced down the nearly deserted highways, the roads were slick with rain. She knew how to get to her old foster home; she just needed to catch up with Boston. He already had a head start.

She was definitely speeding, but she didn't care. Maybe she was reckless. It wasn't just her life she was putting at risk. She knew her men would be pissed, but she couldn't have the weight of Boston's death on her shoulder.

It had been a few hours, and her body shook from the cold. She was tired, wet, cold and scared as she returned to her old home. Boston's bike was on its side in the driveway. Addie left Cowboy's bike the same way, not caring that it was getting scratched.

At that moment, the only thing that mattered was keeping Boston safe.

When Ghost, Cowboy and Ruger walked out of the meeting room to find the front door open and Addie and Dallas missing, their hearts pounded.

Cowboy and Ruger grabbed their guns and investigated while Ghost checked the clubhouse for the girls.

"They're not here," Ghost said as he walked outside.

"Dallas' and my bike are missing," Cowboy cursed as he kicked at the stone on the ground. "It's the middle of the night. Where would they go?"

"I may have told Dallas where Boston was heading," Ghost said as the guilt ate at him.

"If Dallas told Addie, there would be nothing to stop her from following Bos," Ruger sighed as he got onto his bike.

Cowboy took one of the spares before Ghost mounted his own bike. "Where was her last home?" Cowboy couldn't remember, his head running through every scenario.

"Fort Worth," Ruger grumbled, "that's about 3 hours away if they're not speeding."

"She's not equipped to ride in this kind of weather," Cowboy growled, "She's only ridden once."

Their bikes roared to life before they took off. They couldn't have been more than thirty minutes behind the girls. If they were fast enough, they could catch up.

───ℓℓ───

The wind whipped at their skin as they sped down the high-ways, only slowing down when passing the scene of a crash. The lights from the cops and ambulance lit up the dark sky.

As soon as they passed the accident, they fell into line, racing to get to their girls.

They needed to get to them before something terrible hap-pened. Cowboy couldn't help the anxiety gnawing at him.

───ℓℓ───

The front door creaked as she pushed it open. The overwhelm-ing scent of cigarettes and beer assaulted her senses. Her eyes watered at the all-too-familiar stench.

She hoped never to step into this house again, but here she was. She was facing her demons.

She drew her gun out as she swept through the first floor, not finding anyone. Her only choices were the second floor or the basement.

When she noticed the pool of blood in the hallway leading to the basement, her decision was made.

The floor creaked under her weight. Looking around quickly, she took a deep breath. She could do this for Boston.

"Fuck you," she heard Boston roar from down the basement steps. He was alive.

"Oh, Lyle, that's not a nice way to treat someone who only ever cared for you," the voice from her nightmares replied. Tommy.

Her body swayed as she worked her way down the stairs. She knew the layout of the basement more than she wanted to admit.

It was where her bedroom was when she lived here. She was treated like some sort of dog. Not good enough to have in the rest of the home.

Water trailed behind Addie as she walked. The squeaking of her wet boots on the stairs had called the attention of Tommy. His eyes peaking behind his shoulder at Addie.

He saw the gun in her shaking hand and smirked widely.

"Lovely to see you again, Adelynne," Tommy said with a deep chuckle. Addie didn't flinch at his words, not giving him the satisfaction.

Addie looked past Tommy to Boston. He was tied to a chair in the middle of the room, blood pouring from a head wound. His glasses were bent, but he could still see.

She wasn't supposed to follow him. She was supposed to be a good girl and stay at home. So many things he wanted to say to the girl.

Tommy was confused as to why Addie was here, why Boston was here, but it soon clicked, and the man couldn't help but to laugh again.

"What are the chances?" he asked the room, "two of my prized possessions meeting one another?"

Boston growled at that, "She's not a possession. You do not own her."

"Possessive much? Huh? I'd be possessive too with a pussy like that." Tommy hashed back as he made his way over to Addie.

"Don't come any closer, I'll shoot," she warned.

"I'm surprised you didn't tell Lyle about me sooner. But I'm sure he wouldn't have believed you, just like you didn't believe Zoe, right?" He turned his back to Addie to face Boston again.

Boston struggled against his restraints, trying to get free. Addie had not realized that Tommy had a knife on him, but when she saw the metal glint in his hand, she switched the safety off on her gun.

"Like mother, like daughter, right?" Tommy taunted.

"You're sick," Boston retaliated as he shifted his body, the chair scraping across the floor.

"This was Zoe's room, right? As was it Addie's," he continued.

Addie was still confused by his earlier comment. "But you believed someone this time. That's why she's here, right? To avenge her mother's death? Or were you trying to play hero for both?"

Her mother? "I don't have a mother," Addie bit out.

"Not anymore. Your little boyfriend here is the reason she's dead. Maybe if someone had believed her words and cries for help, little Adelynne wouldn't have ended up with me."

Her heart stopped beating. Zoe was her mother?

Footsteps came from behind Addie, but she was still staring at a deflated Boston.

"Ah, there's my boy!" Tommy smiled behind Addie. A man stepped from the shadows.

Addie shivered when she saw the boy. He was college-aged now, but she had remembered seeing him on occasion.

"Adelynne?" the man questioned before looking towards his dad. "Zach," she almost threw up there on the spot.

There was no way, but it all started to make sense. Ronnie. Tommy. Zach. They all shared the same eyes.

She crumbled to her knees as she gasped for air. Boston continued to struggle to get out of his restraints. "I always knew where you were, Adelynne," Tommy explained, "I was going to come for you. You just made it easy for me."

A distraction is what they needed to get out of there. And a distraction is what they got.

Ghost, Cowboy, and Ruger came tumbling down the stairs, guns drawn. In a flash, Tommy had a knife to Boston's throat while Zach had a pocket knife to Addie's.

Addie was always meant to be Zach's. That's what Tommy had said. That's what he was preparing her for.

"Drop the knives," Ruger bit out coldly as he looked at the fresh tears in Addie's eyes.

She felt the knife glide across the skin of her throat. Without thinking, she did what she thought was best.

She shot Tommy in the head to save Boston.

Ruger killed Zach to save her.

She switched the safety back on before she curled in a ball away from Zach's body.

She was cold, in soaking wet clothing and on the basement's cement floor.

"Get me out of these," Boston growled to Ghost and Cowboy as he tried to get to Addie.

Knowing that Tommy was the reason she didn't have a mother was killing her. Boston's heart clenched. He nearly had another death on his shoulders. He couldn't handle it if he lost her after losing Zoe.

"We need to go, now," Ruger huffed out as he scooped Addie up.

"Where's Dallas?" Addie asked weakly, "She was just behind me..."

"She wasn't here when we got here. Maybe she went back to the clubhouse." Ghost said with a small smile, "We'll see her soon."

# Chapter

## TWENTY

As they neared the clubhouse, their bikes roaring down the road, the sun started to shine. It was early in the morning, the birds chirping in the trees. Addie knew she was in for it when they arrived home. If they didn't need to give their statements to the police, they would have been home sooner.

Addie was worn out, and the only thing keeping her awake was the wind whipping across her skin. The cut to her throat was barely a scratch, but it still stung.

When Addie hopped off of Cowboy's bike, remembering the kickstand this time, Boston was on her in a second. "Never risk your safety for me. I'll always fight my way back to you," he said as he hugged Addie close to his chest. "I'm never letting you out of my sight again."

"I'm sorry, but I needed to make sure you were safe. You could have died!" Addie's cries were muffled in the fabric of Boston's shirt.

"She's not here," Ghost's voice broke through to the group. Cowboy became fully alert. Where was Dallas?

"Maybe she went home?" Ruger asked, "We've all had a hell of a night."

"She would have called me." Ghost replied as he pulled his phone out of his pocket.

One missed call.

He listened to the voicemail, his hand gripping the phone tightly. "Shit," he cursed as he mounted his bike again, "she's at the hospital."

"You're not going on a bike again," Ruger warned, "Get in the truck, Addie."

It was an order with no room for discussion. Addie and her men followed Ghsot to the nearest hospital where Dallas was.

The group of five were on edge as they waited in the sterile waiting room. The scent of cleaner prickled at Addie's nose. She hated hospitals.

Her knee bounced up and down while she watched Ghost trying to get any information from the nurses and staff. He was told to sit and wait while they figured out what was happening.

After thirty minutes, a man in blood-covered scrubs stepped into the waiting room, looking around for the group of bikers. "Allison Caville's family?" he called out.

Addie sucked in a deep breath as she shook. The man was covered in blood and had a grim look on his face.

The words barely registered for Addie before she hurled into a nearby trash can. Wave after wave of nausea assaulted her body.

"What do you mean she didn't make it?" She heard Ghost growl, his voice getting louder and louder.

Addie felt a hand rub at her back calmly while another held her hair out of her face.

She wiped at her spit and vomit-covered lips with her PJ shirt sleeve. Tears streamed down her face. The ringing in her ears wouldn't stop.

There was no way. Dallas was right behind her.

The realization hit her hard, sending her toppling back over the trash can to unleash another round of vomiting. Dallas was dead.

It was her fault. Dallas wouldn't have gone out in the storm if it wasn't for Addie leaving. She killed her best friend, her sister.

Addie could see Boston and Ruger holding Ghost back through her blurry eyesight, keeping the man on his feet and off his knees. He was angry; he was heartbroken.

Cowboy continued to soothe Addie. His little sister was dead.

When Addie couldn't throw up anymore, Cowboy led her to a chair before squatting in front of her.

"I'll get you some water," he said softly, almost robotically, "then I need to call my parents."

His sister was gone.

Addie didn't know what to say. If she felt like her whole world was being ripped apart, she had no idea how Cowboy wasn't breaking down. It was his sister.

Cowboy moved like a zombie. His main priority right now was taking care of Addie. He needed to focus on something; otherwise, he would break, too.

"Here, sip on this slowly," he ordered. His voice was light as a feather like he was scared Addie would snap.

She took the water bottle with shaking hands, allowing the man to uncap the drink for her.

"I just need to call my parents," he whispered as he sat beside Addie. His arm wrapped around her waist.

He dialled a number he knew by heart, hesitating momentarily before pressing the call button. He allowed the phone to ring and ring. It was early morning, but his parents should be up by now.

"Reuben," his father greeted. Addie could hear the warmth in his voice and knew the man was about to receive the worst kind of news that would change him forever.

"It's Allie, Pa," Cowboy started carefully. He breathed deeply, trying his hardest to stay calm.

"She was in a crash this morning. The doctors and medics did all they could, but she didn't make it through," he continued, pulling Addie closer.

They both heard the phone hit the floor before the older man howled in pain. "Richard! Richard, are you okay? What's going on?" they could hear Pam panic as she rushed into the room.

Richard's sobs continued through the phone line. Gasping for air, he tried to grasp what his son had just told him.

"Allison," his voice croaked as he tried to get his words out, "Allison is dead."

Cowboy swallowed the nausea he was feeling down. He needed to be strong. Addie, Ghost and his parents needed him to be strong. Dallas wouldn't have wanted him to be in pain.

"My baby!" they heard Pam scream, her sobs coming through, "No! No, she can't be!".

Cowboy watched as Ghost slid down the wall across from them, slumping over, his head to his knees.

Boston and Ruger both didn't know what to do. Someone they considered a little sister, more blood than their own blood.

Ruger was thrown back to the night his mother and sister were murdered. The same kind of heartbreak he knew his friends and Addie were dealing with right now. He knew that kind of pain changes people.

Cowboy couldn't hear his parents sobbing any longer. He quietly hung up the phone before pocketing it.

Where do they even begin to heal? They all felt lost.

Cowboy wouldn't let Ghost go home to his apartment, forcing the man to stay at the clubhouse. Addie felt numb. She felt like this was all a messed-up dream that she would wake up from and laugh about one day.

Addie and Ghost were walking around like ghosts, a shell of their former selves. Boston and Ruger were also obviously upset, putting around trying to take care of their friends and lover.

But Cowboy, Cowboy was the worst of them all. He was walking around like nothing had happened.

He was putting his entire focus on everyone else like he was trying to avoid the pain.

Addie stared blankly at the wall. She couldn't help but let the guilt eat at her. She would always know she was the reason Dallas wasn't here.

Dallas would never be coming home.

## TWENTY ONE

C hristmas day seemed a lot colder this year. Though it was bright outside, inside the clubhouse, it was anything but.

Addie couldn't bring herself to look at the tree that Dallas had helped decorate. She couldn't bring herself to look at the presents that the other girl had wrapped. She couldn't bring herself to care about anything.

Thinking about Dallas cut at Addie's heart. Whenever she would go to text or call her best friend, she cried. She broke down in Ghost's arms that morning when she let the man in and realized he had come alone. Right. Dallas was dead.

What was supposed to be a joyous day was one of heartache.

Pam and Richard sat on the couch closest to the illuminated tree, wiping their eyes with tissues as fresh tears bubbled through.

The fire roared in an attempt to warm up the room. The crackling of wood covering the sniffles coming from a few members in the room.

Cowboy was the first one to stand up, walking towards the gifts. He grabbed the gifts wrapped in black, one by one, giving them to the appropriate person.

"Allie would have wanted you guys to have these gifts," he started, "she always loved Christmas. She would hate to have us all crying today."

Addie blinked up at her man as Ruger rubbed at her back in a calming way. Boston sipped on his coffee as he stood in the doorway.

Pam was the first one to attempt to open a gift. Hers was a tennis bracelet engraved with Dallas and Cowboy's birth years. It was simple, yet meant the world to the grieving mother.

Richard was gifted tickets to a football game. Dallas had wanted to go with him. She saved up enough money to surprise the man.

Everyone had tears in their eyes when they opened their gifts from Dallas, and Addie was last. She gently tugged on the black wrapping paper, allowing it to land on the floor by her feet. Inside was a small velvet box.

She lifted the lid slowly, taking a moment to take the piece of jewelry in. It was a simple yellow-gold chain with a single circular pendant. Stamped on the charm were two flowers: a daffodil and a lily of the valley.

Most people wouldn't have known what it meant, but Addie did. They represented her children—a daffodil for her baby boy, who would have been born in March. The yellow flower represented hope and joy.

Lily-of-the-valley represented the child she was carrying. According to her doctor, her due date would be in May—the white flower represented a return to happiness.

"That's beautiful," Ruger commented, "what does the note say?". Inside the box was a small note. Addie pulled the piece of paper out before reading the words.

*'For my nephew and the sweet babe on the way. Auntie will always love you.'*

A fresh wave of tears hit as Addie's hands shook. Boston set his mug down on the coffee table before approaching Addie. He took the piece of paper out of her hand before reading it himself. A sad smile crossed his face before he handed the paper to Cowboy.

"She loved them more than you could have known," Ghost explained as he looked over at Addie, "She was so excited. I'm sorry she won't be here for you".

Addie shook her head as she hiccuped. This was the most thoughtful gift anyone had ever given her.

Everyone besides Richard and Pam looked sullen at the note, the parents not understanding. "She was so excited for us to tell you," Cowboy turned to his parents, "Addie is pregnant. Due in May".

Even though he was grieving, he was still a proud father. "Allie bought her a necklace with what would have been her son's birth month and then a flower for this baby's due date," he explained.

Pam let out another sob. She felt like her heart was being ripped out and sewn back together all at once. She was going to be a grandmother. "Please let me know if you ever need anything, sweetheart," Pam said with a small smile on her face. Tears were still present in her eyes, but she looked at Addie with so much love.

"You already were, but I just want to say it: you're family," Richard said as he held his wife close.

Everyone stumbled through Christmas, all just going through the motions. There were some laughs and pure happiness throughout the day and night. Some moments when it didn't feel like they had lost someone so important. It was nice. Dallas would have been happy.

Pam and Addie baked cookies, all different kinds. The two of them chatted about life and their hopes for the future. There were tears, but it was good not to be trapped in their own heads.

The guys hadn't touched their bikes since the day of the accident, and none had returned to work yet. It didn't feel right. Boston said they needed time to grieve. They had it all planned out. They could mope around until New Year's Eve, but after that, they would get back on with life.

Dallas would have been kicking their asses already for all the tears and heartbreaking sadness in the air. It felt so heavy now, just the world's weight on their shoulders. But they would heal.

They had to. They couldn't allow this to be the end for them all.

Cowboy could swear he heard Dallas cussing him out for allowing Addie to be sad.

The man watched on as Addie and Pam got covered in flour as they baked their sadness away. They were finally breathing for the first time in a week since Dallas had gotten into her accident—a week without one of his favourite people.

"We'll be okay," Ruger assured, "Dallas needs us to be. Our baby needs us to be... And Addie, Addie won't survive if we don't stay strong".

"I know, Ruger. I'm doing what I can to stay strong. For both of them.".

"That's not what I mean, Reuben," Ruger sighed heavily, "you need to grieve, too. You can't be a superhero for everyone. But you cannot allow yourself to fester in the darkness. I know what it's like. It's not easy, but we need you."

Boston was finally at a loss. He wasn't around when Ruger lost his mother and sister. He didn't know what it was like. He didn't know what to do to help. It was his responsibility to fix things, and this was just something he couldn't fix.

## TWENTY TWO

A nger reverberated off Addie's body as she glared at the man she thought she loved.

Cowboy.

Ruger and Boston watched on in silence, their jaws tense as they watched the two fighting.

"You're telling me to move on?" She growled, "She was my best friend. Your fucking sister. Your flesh and blood, and I seem to care more about her death than you!"

Cowboy flinched at the anger from his lover. His everything. The mother of their child.

"I do care, Addie," he replied quietly. His heart continued to break.

"If you cared, you would be just as heartbroken or more! I just want it to stop hurting. It hurts, and hurts, and hurts. It feels like

I can't breathe anymore. I want it to stop hurting. I want to stop hurting. I want to be numb."

"You need me. The boys need me. Our baby needs me," he stressed, "Dallas needed me, and I couldn't protect her. I cannot allow myself to grieve the way you are grieving because I can't risk you all losing me, too. That should have been me chasing you, not Dallas."

Addie's eyes softened as she realized how venomous her words had become. "Cowboy, I didn't..."

Cowboy crowded around her as his hands reached for her face carefully, "I'm so fucking depressed that my sister is dead. That I could have maybe prevented it. I blame myself with every breath I breathe, knowing it should have been me in that casket, not her".

Addie attempted to say something else, but Cowboy cut her off. "No, you need to know. You need to listen."

"She would have done anything to save you both... because she loved you. Because you're family. Because we love you".

*"Because we love you".*

If love could have saved anyone, Allison Montgomery Caville would still be there with them.

# Thank You

I have so many people I want to thank for helping me turn my dream into reality.

Thank you to my Dad for being my biggest supporter and for keeping the "haters" in line. I know our lives have been a little crazy, but I truly appreciate all of the love and support you've given me. Thank you for always being my cheerleader. I was a little nervous you didn't quite understand what a spicy romance book entailed, but you didn't care and wanted to tell everyone about my book.

Thank you to my brother, Brandon, for supporting my smutty writing and giving me some good laughs along the way. You better not have read this book... If you did, do NOT tell me!

Courtney, thank you for torturing my brother with this book; I'm sure you've been quoting some of the more dirty lines to make him uncomfortable. I love you!

Carol, you're always so supportive of me and love me through everything. I'm just going to pretend you haven't read this book, though.

Kim, I hope you and your friend enjoyed this book on your trip! Thanks for being supportive of this dream of mine.

Damien, thank you for being so supportive through this whole process. It means the world to me.

Heather, Devon, and Jamie, thank you for being the reason this book actually came to life. Without you, I would have just pushed the thoughts of writing and publishing this book away.

Kelly, you're the baddest bitch I've ever met. You always hype me up, no matter what. I love you so much.

Lexie, Melissa, and Steph, thank you for supporting me even when I don't talk to you guys for weeks at a time. I've been stuck in book mode for a few months. I love you guys.

Hannah and Emily, thank you for everything. I love you both like family.

Thank you to K.B. Barrett for the amazing covers and chapter headings. You were a dream to work with and helped me learn a lot more about publishing books. You helped me by holding my hand through the whole process, and I couldn't have been more grateful for you.

Thank you to everyone on TikTok who believed in this silly little dream of mine.

Lastly, thank you to my amazing husband, Rob, who loved and supported me through this wild ride. You helped me more than you could imagine. Your support right off the bat until the end has been incredible, and I will always be thankful for you. I love you. To the moon and back.

# Also by the Author

Coming April 2024

**Wine and Leather by Daina Edwards**

*After a lifetime of misery, Addie finally found refuge*

*But then, unimaginable tragedy strikes once more*

Everyone at Rising Tide MC is mourning the loss of sweet, beautiful Dallas – and nobody is more devastated than Addie and Cowboy, Dallas' big brother. Addie keeps blaming herself for her best friend's death while Cowboy struggles to accept the truth.

Can a new life heal the loss of another? It's a question that fills Addie with dread, especially with her wound still so raw.

This time, the journey to find the light at the end of the tunnel is met with numerous detours. But with her three Rising Tide members by her side – fearless club president Boston, dependable ex-marine Ruger, and sweet, loyal Cowboy – Addie is once again geared up to fight for her and her baby's happiness.

Tik Tok: dainaedwardsauthor
Instagram: dainaedwardsauthor
Facebook: Daina Edwards Romance Author